BECOMING THE CONJURER

Nick Oliveri

BECOMING THE CONJURER

A NOVEL BY NICK OLIVERI

Nick Oliveri

Copyright © 2023 Nicholas Oliveri
All rights reserved.

The characters and events portrayed in this book are fictitious. Any similarity to real persons, living or dead, is coincidental and not intended by the author.

No part of this book may be reproduced, or stored in a retrieval system, or transmitted in any form or by any means, electronic, mechanical, photocopying, recording, or otherwise, without express written permission of the publisher.

ISBN: 979-8-374604-58-0

Becoming The Conjurer

More Books by Nick Oliveri

The Conjurer
The Last Conjurer
Monsters in My Mind
A Genocide Too Small
Her
A Boy Just Like Me
Oxycodone And Her Canvas

Nick Oliveri

To The Conjurers of the world. May they be responsible with their power and influence.

Becoming The Conjurer

The Conjurer—the being who creates and tells the stories that define the kingdom and the minds that comprise it.

The Conjurer pulls the heartstrings of the commoners perfectly, acutely, and pristinely. He fine-tunes his message to make people *believe*.

The King of Idaza crafts decisions. The Secretary to the king makes suggestions. The merchant deals in currency while the potter works in clay. **But The Conjurer deals in belief**—belief in the traditions, policies, social institutions, and very infrastructure of the celebrated and spotless nation of Idaza. The Conjurer makes the stories the commoners have in their hearts as they while away at work in the fields, the bustling streets, and in artisan craft shops.

The Chief of Coin enlists the help of The Conjurer to persuade people to pay taxes to the wise and discerning state. The Head of Education relies on The Conjurer to instill the lore of Idaza's glorious and righteous past in young minds. Finally, the Commander of the Military relies on The Conjurer to encourage Idaza's many little hands to play with spears rather than toys and pens.

The world spins and swings and revolves around the tales of The Conjurer—his stories, shadows, and words spun and spoken in the purest gold. The Conjurer

gives the markets their money, the spears their wielding hands, and the sandals their springing feet.
>He is the spirit.
>He is the guide.
>He is the story.

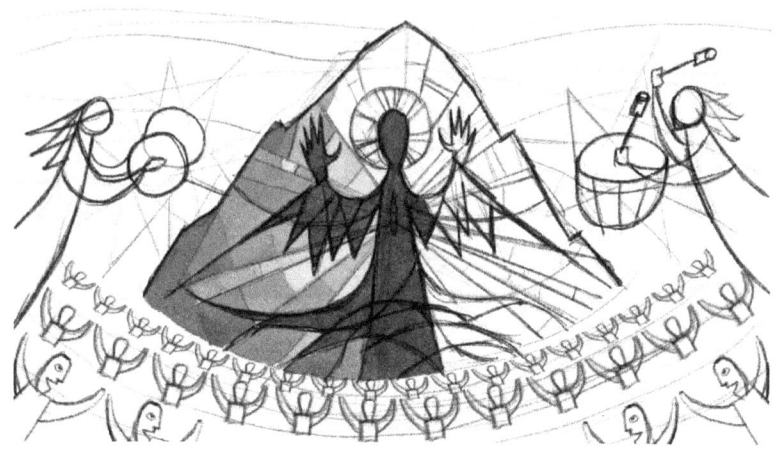

Prologue

The bloodline of the Menizaks was pure. The Menizaks ruled over Idaza with care and strength and a certain boldness of heart that united the commoners and nobles, the peasants and warriors, and all the rest. Menizak IV was the prince and the heir to the throne that his father, Menizak III, held. He had a helmet on, emblazoned with gold and silver, so only his fearsome eyes shone through. He was tall and fit, bound with tight muscles all across his body. He held his spear in his hand with white knuckles. He stood resolute, awaiting the entrance of his father into the palace foyer so they could depart together into battle. It was a grand entrance with a vaulted ceiling right near the front of the palace. A chandelier of gold and many flames hung in the air. And then, with steps of clapping thunder and the clank of a spear's touch to marble, Menizak IV's father strode toward him.

"I'm ready, father."

"I know you are." And then the great man stepped back and squinted at his son in his helmet and armor. "You look like a warrior."

"I *am* a warrior."

"Of course you are. You're a Menizak."

They both looked in one another's eyes with a steely certainty—some sacred bond between a father and his firstborn, brothers in battle, a royal connection.

After a pause and a couple of breaths, the great man smacked the brunt of his spear against his marble floor, creating a huge sound that echoed among the many palace halls. "Then let us leave, let us lead, and by the gods, let us never relent. To battle, my son."

"To battle."

But like some childish harbinger, the soft pelting of small footsteps scattered throughout the halls coming closer to the pair in the foyer.

"Let's just leave," said Menizak IV, already tensing up at the sound, anxiety spreading across his face and chest.

"Hold on," his father said.

And right then, a boy walked in. Driveled all over his face was the soft pudge of high status, fleshy cheeks, tanned skin from sitting in the sun, and noodly arms from years of childish lounging.

"Oro," the king said, "what are you doing? You need to get ready for school."

"I know, father. But I just wanted to see you before you left for your campaign." The boy bubbled with joy at seeing his brave father prepare for battle.

Becoming The Conjurer

Look how strong he is. Look at his muscles and that armor. When I grow up, I want to be just like my father. Oro looked up, way up, at his father, beaming all the way.

He desired to be a "Menizak" more than anything else in the world. But he wasn't the firstborn, and he wasn't strong like them. He didn't have wild eyes like them. He didn't have his father's muscle mass or his brother's ferocity. Instead, he had a big heart and a soft soul that bled too easily.

"Go to school, Oro." Menizak IV looked at Oro with snide disdain, a mocking smirk spreading across his lips. "Go learn how to be a courtier or something. Maybe even learn how to be a farmer."

"Boys, that's enough. We are one house and we must not forget that. Menizak, leave now. I will follow you in a moment."

The younger Menizak said, "pudgy," as he grabbed his spear and left. A vicious parting shot.

Pangs hit Oro's gut and watered his eyes. He turned his face away from his noble father, covering it with his hands to conceal his weakness from the king.

"What's wrong, Oro?" His father put a giant hand on his shoulder. "You know your brother is harsh, but he loves you. Plus, you're not fat; he just likes to say it because he's your brother."

Oro sobbed, taking his hands off his face. "It's just... It's just—"

"It's just what?"

Still crying, Oro explained his tears in the exact words that hurt him so deeply. "It's just that I'll... *I'll never be you guys.* I'll never be anyone. My brother hates me because, well, I don't know why!"

"Hey," his father said in a soft voice, kneeling now to meet Oro's eyes, "he doesn't hate you. On the contrary, he loves you, Oro, very much. As do I. I'll always be your father, and I'll always love you. But he has the spirit of Menizak in him. He is the first prince, the one to bind and control our whole great nation, and I need to pass on everything I know to him. I know you understand that, Oro. Now, please, get to school and remind everyone why you're a prince as well, my son." And with that, Menizak III took his spear and headed toward the door.

"He's better than me," Oro said, his voice cracking.

His father just looked at him from behind as he took off out the door, saying nothing and staring blankly at his son.

Oro watched his father leave the palace and whispered painfully to himself. "He's better than me."

Chapter 1

His face flickered in the light of the flame. His forehead glowed gold, and his cheekbones were tinted a harsh red. A dance of wavering energy flared and flashed, illuminating Mikalla's solemn face. His vast room was vacant and dark, cave-like, with him as the only occupant, alone in his chair and staring at the candle's flame on his desk, which seemed to live and breathe. He didn't quite know why, but he felt alone. Hopelessly alone and misunderstood.

The flame allowed for the glow of the single tear that stroked his cheek, streaming from his desperate, stolid eyes. The tear rolled on, down to his protruding jawline, and jumped off into the abyss below, falling and falling until it splashed into nothingness.

He wished someone could hear his whispering tears. But they were quiet, hushed in the dark, singed into silence by the biting heat of the flame. There was no one to care or hear his cry. Not a single soul could comprehend the hurt inside him. This made the pain worse, and the pain made him lonelier. He sat in his chair

and eventually got into bed, his mind attacking him with every step and breath.
But on the following day, the sun shone over the kingdom of Idaza once more.

***

"Mikalla! Breakfast is ready!" His mother yelled up to him from downstairs. A servant walked into his room.

"Master Mikalla, your meal awaits you in the kitchen."

Unlike most of the other nobles, Mikalla's house was modestly sized, although he had some of the amenities that a noble may expect to have—running water, servants, and the like. His family was of the lower nobility—neither rich nor poor, and both his honorable parents had stable jobs in the government.

"Good morning, Miki." His mother caressed the boy in her arms after he reached the bottom of the stairs. Mikalla was short for a thirteen-year-old, and his mother had to bend down just to hug him. "How did you sleep?"

"Pretty well," Mikalla said, looking away. "Where's father?"

"He already left for work. Why don't you sit down and eat your avocado? I know they're your favorites."

"I need the sauce."

"It's already on the table. Unfortunately, I have to leave soon for work too."

"Okay," Mikalla said, looking down at the food. His face drooped. Blank. Hurt.

"How was school yesterday? Did you have a good day? I had to work late again."

"It was fine."

Mikalla's mother stared at the boy, who was just flicking his food around with his fork. Her brows furrowed and her chin drooped. "Is everything okay?" Her hand reached over and placed itself as gently as cotton on Mikalla's bony shoulder. Slowly, back and forth, she rubbed and caressed the back of his neck and the top of his head. The boy tried to turn away, run away, even. But instead of leaving, he stayed right in his chair and absorbed his mother's warm embrace.

"No. Not really."

"Are you sure, Miki? Are you being treated well?"

"I guess so," he said, mumbling and staring down at his untouched breakfast.

"Well, you only get to go to school with the royal family and the higher nobles because of a privilege you earned for your talents. You're very smart, Miki—so, so smart. I wouldn't be surprised if those snobby royals were jealous of your talent."

He sighed. "Yeah, I know."

"Hey, look at me." His mother's eyes and jaw sharpened into a beautiful fury. She looked solemnly and slowly, like a panther, into Mikalla's burning eyes. Her mad voice fell to a violent whisper, soft, slow, and hushed. "You're stronger than you think, Mikalla. You're greater than you know. Just keep speaking from your heart, and your path will reveal itself."

"But I don't want my path to be some priest's or some clerk's like yours and dad's. They tell me it's a privilege to go there, but where's the privilege if I can't choose?"

And then his mother's bright eyes loomed stormier as the sunlight faded to dark clouds. "You sound selfish right now. You have no idea how lucky you are. How about you take a trip to the city commons and see how most of our kingdom lives?"

"I wouldn't do that because there's nothing to look at down there," Mikalla said. "They don't have sculptures and paintings like up here. They don't know what beauty is."

"How would you know that if you've never tried?" His mother asked, trying to play to her son's reasoning.

"Because I know, Mother! It's dirty down there. It's loud and vulgar. I want culture, and if I can't find it up here, I certainly won't be able to find it down there."

His mother liked to play mind games to test Mikalla's reactions by throwing out comments. Finally, she turned away from Mikalla so he could not see her face and cracked a smirk. "You're sounding more and more like a clerk every day."

And at that snide remark, Mikalla felt a torrent of rage and anguish bubble up. It was a fiery impulse, one that swore him into a reddened rage—a spewing stew of white-hot blood. "You don't know anything, mother! When I grow up, I want to be The Conjurer!"

His mother gasped. Her eyes widened like giant, dark tunnels. "Mikalla! Do *not* say that out loud! You know better than that." She then strode to the nearest window to make sure nobody outside heard what his son uttered. "Don't say that again, please. You know what that job means."

And what his mother said was true. The job of The Conjurer meant everything to the people of Idaza, to the nobles, and even to the king himself. It was taken more seriously—and more spiritually—than any other position in all of the kingdom. The Conjurer was a tool for the king. The Conjurer provided meaning for the people and entertainment for the nobility. It was the only job that tied all of Idaza together, and there could only be one at a time. Every week, there would be one ceremony, in which the commoners would pack into the Idazan stadium situated and carved beside a mountain.

Then, The Conjurer and their crew would work to tell stories to the masses using shadow puppets cast by the giant ceremonial flame.

Mikalla stared down at his avocado plate. He mumbled something in a low, tired breath.

"What was that?" His mother asked.

He mumbled again. This time, he was louder, with his lips buzzing and tongue lashing.

"Mikalla, speak up, please."

"It was nothing, mother."

"Say it."

Mikalla inhaled for a minute. His mother had a stone face, was stern and calm, serene and determined. "I do know what that job means. And that's why I want it."

His mother got closer, bending down to meet his eyes. Grace left her as anger refilled her face with splotches of red. "Do *not* talk like that outside of this house. Do you know what could happen to us or to *you* if you're found talking about that? About The Conjurer? That position? It's sacred, Mikalla. You're a lower noble; you don't have access to that position. Besides, they've already probably chosen multiple successors, each person trained from a baby to become The Conjurer. It's a life you weren't born into."

Mikalla shivered and saw the passing flashes of greatness and rejection, flames, and mad crowds moving like a tidal wave at the whim of his hand. He felt that it could all be his, but his mother didn't seem to think that was possible—no one did. "And who's" *'they'*?"

"The ones that choose The Conjurer. They train him."

"Yeah," said Mikalla, "and who are they?"

"Mikalla," his mom said and sighed, "I don't know. But I do know you ask a lot of questions for a boy who's about to be late for school."

As he gathered his things and gave his wooden dish to the servant, he turned back toward his mother. "I really want to know who they are."

His mother sent him on his way, nudging the back of his shoulders and neck gingerly with her hand and prodding him out the door.

"We're not supposed to know."

Chapter 2

Pink twilight painted a canvas of sky. A boy named Kitan swept the dusty streets. He walked alone. He swept alone. The scratch of the broom was the only sound as the dimness of night seeped through the many walkways of the city commons. His long, spidery fingers held a splintery broom handle. His sharp eyes focused on the dirt and dust below, but his mind went elsewhere. He liked to think about great worlds where the people had no hierarchy.

The boy liked to envision a bigger, broader world, where the streets were always clean and the handles of things didn't have splinters. He swept almost every night, as was his job. Still, with the sound of the scratching broom sweeping the path, he looked up at the sky and wondered. He wondered if his crazy ideas were possible or if they were even his. He wondered about time and all of its fickle elements, and how to better harness it. *So much could be done about this city*, he thought. *So much could be done for this city. For these people. My job could be easier. This life could be easier. Somewhere, or at some point, maybe it already is.*

And then, as he gazed up at the fading pink-painted sky, he heard footsteps approach. They were careful and steady. They were calm but determined. He lurched his head around and darted his eyes. But nothing appeared. Nothing came about. *Where are those coming from?* He looked around more. He stopped breathing, stopped sweeping, and stopped stepping. He hunched his neck and head and tried his best to open his ears. He tried his best to locate the sound of the footsteps.

Are they around the corner?

He heard them getting closer. *Clop clop. Clop clop.* The hard bottom of well-made sandals was a rich sound on the stone walkway, and it stayed steady and fixed, approaching and coming yet closer, still out of sight.

Clop clop. Clop clop.

"Hello?" Kitan said. His voice cracked. "Uhm, anybody there?" He shivered as the night fell upon him. The pink turned into a rich black blanket of sky that stretched down to the ground. Everything grew dark, crisp, and cold.

Kitan dropped the broom, and a splinter speared his hand. He didn't notice it. He backed into a wall and said again, "Hello?"

This time, a figure cloaked in the blanket of night appeared out of the bend of the walkway, around a turn, and heading toward Kitan. Kitan, just a teenager, tried to speak, but his voice was choked. His back was against the wall.

Clop clop. The figure got larger, and Kitan gasped, silently failing to gulp the night air.

He could then make the figure out more clearly—dark robes and a clean-cut face, moonlight gleaming off the gold on his wrists and neck. He continued to walk until he stepped on the broom in the middle of the street. It snapped like a weak and splintered twig. But the nobleman didn't seem to care or notice. He just continued to walk and stare ahead, sandals kicking up dirt along the way, making a mess of the path that Kitan had just cleaned.

With sharp, determined eyes, Kitan watched the nobleman walk away and turn the next corner of the street path. The teenager—in a tattered robe—picked up his snapped broom, holding one piece in each hand. As his heart rate and breathing eased, he noticed a long splinter in his left hand with growing redness around the wound. He looked around at all the dirt sprinkled and sprayed throughout. The street looked as if he had never swept at all.

The night was as black as the ocean's great plunge. He let the street lamps guide the way to his home after he sighed at the dirt spread at his feet.

Simply alone in his hut, he lit his candles after his eyes adjusted to the void of darkness. He scratched his head and sat at his only table. By the light of the flickering candle, a set of objects appeared spread across his desk, scattered but somehow having some purpose. From the top-down, it appeared to be a city—made of chips of wood and stone and clay. It resembled loosely the kingdom of Idaza but had additions of tracks and wire that connected street markets and people and homes. The tracks had wheeled vehicles carved from wood, and the wires—made from cloth string—had small objects that resembled pails clinging to and grating across the strings, delivering goods to homes and markets. It was like Idaza but easier. It was like Idaza, but quicker. It was Idaza, but better connected.

Kitan, still with the splinter in his hand, revealed his face by the flickering candlelight, and his eyes' sharpness melted to a smooth and light joy. He looked at his splinter, wincing as he pulled it out. He glanced at the broken broom in the corner of the room. He winced again.

His job was so inefficient. He was always being stepped on—just like the broom he had, snapped in half. That's how it made him feel—snapped in half. He had no agency. As a lowly commoner, he was unable to build anything worthwhile. All he could do was clean up what was already made.

He was sick of it and sick of the life he had. He yearned for a status where he could influence things, notice things, and *build* things. He saw, in his mind, a kingdom that was always clean and needed no brooms. He saw a faster kingdom, a kingdom where no one would have to sweep or clean much, and be stepped on by others that had more. Everyone could have more and *be* more.

This is what Kitan saw. This is what he wanted. This is what the model on his rickety table meant. And it meant more to him than anyone or anything.

Orphaned. Unlike the snapped broom, his vision was the only thing intact.

Chapter 3

The high school was packed and orderly. Gold covered the walls in ornate patterns, and columns of ivory bound down every regal hallway. All the children had robes of fine red and yellow silk and were adorned with gold bracelets and fine leather sandals. That was, all the children except Mikalla. Mikalla sat in the back of the class behind a girl with long, dark hair.

He just looked straight ahead and listened to the teacher speak, often finding that his eyes wandered to the silk clothing and fine, hand-crafted jewelry of the other students. After all, like sticky humidity on a summer's day, Mikalla's eye was drawn to the bright and the lustrous, the gold and the silver, the paintings and the etchings of the best that life had to offer.

"Alright everyone, later today we have a special guest coming in from the high court," the teacher said, as a chorus of gasps arose from the students. The teacher, Master Chapauhtli, had a long, rodent-like face and bowing yellow teeth like shriveled fangs. Mischief laced his small green eyes. "Now, this is nothing to be alarmed about. It is simply for him to get to know you better as students. That is all. We will be expecting him in the afternoon, and this day may go until after hours."

Great. Another reason to cast me aside, Mikalla thought to himself. He held his skinny chin in his hands as the teacher continued with the first lesson of the day.

***

Kitan awoke the next day tired after an onslaught of nightmares. He stumbled out of bed, putting on one of the only two robes he owned before reporting to his post to get sanitation instructions for the day ahead.

"Kittral," his boss said, "you're assigned something different today."

"My name's... Kitan."

"Yes, yes, okay. But I'm sending you to a schoolhouse today. You're on bathroom duty."

Kitan just sat there while his stomach churned into a swirling storm. "Like, the schoolhouse by the central market plaza?"

His boss, taller, bigger, and hairier than him, stepped closer and looked down at the lonely boy. "No," he said, "the one in the Inner Gardens—the high noble academy."

Kitan nearly threw up. Bulging eyes quaked underneath the teenager's wrinkling forehead. "Like, the school where the prince goes?"

"Yes. That school. But that doesn't concern you. The guards at the edge of the Inner Gardens will know what you mean if you tell them you're there to clean—I've already briefed them. Just give them your name, and they will escort you to your post for the day."

Kitan tried to hide his shaking body. He had only ever seen a couple nobles in his life, and they had never seen him before. He thought of the black-clad man from the night before and shuddered. He turned around to skitter to his job for the day.

"It might take until sundown today. Oh, and bring that broom back by sundown."

***

The girl with the long and dark hair in front of Mikalla was the next to be called to meet with the official. She wore a smile of triumph.

"Jani, you're next," the teacher said. And with that, Jani strode quickly out of the room and out of sight of Mikalla's curious eyes. The teacher continued with the lesson on history and lore and the irreducibly complex and mundane workings of the Idazan government, ultimately ending with the idea that the king's rule was divine and final. The more the teacher spoke about the Idazan government, the more eyes in the classroom floated to the front of the room, sticking to the pudgy figure sitting in a specially-cushioned chair. The prince attracted immense attention—feces to flies. He had a stroke of innocence painted across his tanned skin and boyish face. Mikalla and the rest of the students knew him as Oro, Prince of Idaza and second in line to the throne, under his brother, Menizak IV.

Jani walked away from the class, the lone student trailing the high court official like a human tail. "Where are you taking me?" she asked.

"Just to one of the conference rooms," the official said. They kept walking down the many pillared halls and gold-gilded walls.

"What is this for?" Jani asked. "And why are you here?"

The official sighed quietly to himself as he looked ahead and walked on. "I'm here by a royal decree of His Highness. I have a job to do."

"You mean my uncle? Yeah, he's quite something."

The official—tall and bony under a long, white silk robe—sighed again. "Yes, your uncle, Jani, who is also the King of Idaza."

The official ushered Jani into a room with no window to the outside, no natural light, and only candles and lamps for them to see. "So what are we doing here?"

"Just a little test—I mean, interview."

"A test? Well, I have no doubt I'll pass."

"I said interview."

"You said 'test' before it," Jani said. She had cat-shaped eyes that lent to her fox-like demeanor. She was aggressive and smooth. She looked up at the bony official insistently and sneakily. Pressing forward, Jani asked, "What are you looking for? What's the point?"

"I'm not supposed to say that, Jani." Then, like the deep and throaty belch of a bullfrog, the official laughed to himself. "This isn't a normal test. And this certainly isn't a normal interview."

Chapter 4

Kitan arrived at the Inner Gardens, and at the sight of the high walls and stern guards, his jaw tightened. The guard, clothed in some gray uniform, looked him up and down and tried to find the prick of a certain mannerism to instill fear in the young sanitation worker. He could find none. Kitan looked back at the guard in a heat of cold indifference, with a certain look that seemed to say, *I'm here for a job.*

"Name!" the guard growled, still glaring at Kitan.

"Kitan. I'm cleaning the bathrooms of the high noble schoolhouse today."

After a grunt, the guard stepped aside. "Right this way."

His eyes jumped around hastily as he followed the guard through the Inner Gardens, devouring the sight of shining robes and ivory statues of heroic figures, big marble structures, ornate carvings in clay, oak, and gold, and short green plants and grass.

How inefficient! How many resources are going here? How many people like me are working to maintain these? How many slaves do this work? How much money? How much time? A violent, gurgling pulse churned his stomach when he saw fine, small stones inlaid like a flawless checkerboard in a boundless field of freshly cut grass so pure that it was nearly blue in the sheen of the morning sun.

They approached the high, noble schoolhouse, marble and gold and shimmering like a live statue, a great plaque commemorating only the best Idaza had to offer. They walked on toward the royal school. *Why the jewels? Why the silk? Why the marble and gold? If I could only grab a small chunk of this, a tiny morsel of gold, I could begin to build. I could begin to actualize my vision, the true world. The future of Idaza is near; I just know it. Then these people would realize....*

"Okay," the guard said, "this is the end of the line for me. There's a head janitor in there to the right that will show you around and give you the rest of what you need. Do *not, under any circumstances*," the guard squinted and scowled at the shorter boy, "think of speaking to *anyone*. Not the students. Not the teachers. And no one else, either. You will keep your head down and do what you're told," the guard said, gritting his horrendous, wolf-like teeth, "or you will give up your head in the name of His Highness." Kitan walked inside, not taking his careful, hungry eyes off the gold stripes or the giant marble pillars that stood everywhere. He'd only been to school for a few years before loathing the whole idea of it to death. *But this school could have worked for me.*

As the guard disappeared out the main entrance, Kitan sank further into the bowels of towering white marble until he came upon a peculiar sight. His eyes struck two people walking by. One was a man, tall and draped in fine white silk, and another—a dark-haired girl—tailed shortly and quickly behind. He felt the urge to speak—to say something, anything, to get their attention. He observed a possibility so great ahead of him that he disregarded the risk. He was not much older than the dark-haired girl.

"Uhm, hi, hello, where is the head janitor?"

The tall official in white took one look at the teen in tattered robes, scoffed, and walked right past him. He escorted the girl away and into a windowless room, where they continued to talk.

Kitan, like a lost duckling alone, took strides toward a back corridor away from the main hallway. "Hello?" he said to no one. Speaking into the void to soothe an itch and a duty he had to fulfill. He wandered alone and with each step grew angrier and more alone down the many spidery corridors.

Kitan noticed cobwebs growing in the corners of the hallways which narrowed at every corner and turn. "Hello? Is there a head janitor here? It's me, Kitan. I'm here to clean on behalf of..." and he just sighed. No one could hear him. No one cared to hear him.

***

Mikalla sat in the back and zoned out—from the lesson, from everything. A cloud surrounded his head the more he was left alone, and the more that cloud came and thundered, the more he wanted to be by himself. Looking around at the silk and the bracelets made him feel like he was thrown into a life he never asked for. Like a pestle thrown into the fire, it was unable to escape, shout, or do much of anything except burn to cinders and turn back into brown earth.

He was a creature, alien to what he was supposed to know so well—each day a new and bright slog through a dark path to a destination he never wanted. He needed a spark. But he'd get that spark sooner than he'd ever hoped to expect.

He saw that Oro the Prince was out of his seat as well. *Of course, the prince gets to do what he wants and go wherever he pleases. But for me? What do I get? I get to sit in my seat and stay here against my will until I grow old enough to be a government clerk.*

But in a stroke of luck, the girl with the dark hair returned to her seat. She was no longer smiling. *Oh gods, what did they do to her? What does this official want from us? With me?* Mikalla felt the pang of anxious tendrils creep up and grip his chest and neck. His ruby heart pounded wildly. His feet felt heavy, and his palms were saturated with thick sweat. Smoke filled his vision and his ears roused an alarm as he heard his name.

"Mikalla." The teacher said it in a gruff voice. "Mikalla! Don't let me say it again! You're next to meet with the official."

He shot up sharply out of instinct. "Yes? Yeah. Sorry. And where do I go again?"

"Down to the left and in the meeting room. The first one. You won't miss it," the instructor said with sharp eyes intent on the lower noble boy.

The official sat among a gorge of flames consuming the air, gurgling silently in the dark. Only his eyes seemed to shine. "Sit down, Mikalla."

"Y-you know my name?"

"Only because your instructor gave it to me. Now sit down." Mikalla shivered. "You're a lower noble, correct?"

"I guess so." Mikalla stared at the ground. The chasm looked back at him.

"What do you mean, 'I guess so?'"

"Yes. I'm a lower noble." The words stung Mikalla.

"Okay, let's get this over with." The official took a satchel from the side of the room and placed it on the table. He removed a lone cacao bean and placed the bag back on the ground. The bean made a tiny, clacking sound.

What is this? Mikalla thought. *Why is he looking at me like that? That's the commoners' money on the table—what is he doing with that?*

The official lit a candle on the table. The flame danced, and the bean on the table followed its lead, mesmerized and entranced. One and one from two different worlds collided in a meld of sameness: the bean and the candle's gasping energy force. Mikalla just stared.

"This," the official said, holding up the cacao bean, "is an important commodity for the commoners. It's a uniform asset that they use to barter between unlike goods—a currency. Yes, the cacao bean is a currency." The official's voice went higher, and his eyes danced with the flame, revealing a white crescent smile. "What is this currency to you? What is this currency to the king, His Highness? What is this currency to the kingdom as a whole?" He put the bean back down and kept smiling bleakly and grimly across the table at Mikalla, who had his eyes intent on the bean.

What the hell is going on? Is this a trick? A simple prank to laugh at me? Or is this really a test? And if it's a test, what do I get if I pass? Mikalla pictured Jani and the other students giving mundane and thoughtless answers. Haphazard and spoiled people speak in the same vein. Mikalla pictured his future, buried in the countless scrolls scrawled with etchings everywhere. Seeing those etchings in his dreams as a government clerk crushed him and made his insides tense up with disgust.

But that couldn't be his life. That couldn't be his pursuit. He knew that somewhere, buried between the cells that pumped in the blood of his veins, there was a flame ignited by the unknown that could be extinguished by nothing. He decided, for a change, to let that flame light the way.

"Hey, hey, Mikalla, snap out of it. I asked you a question. Remember the bean? What is it? What does it mean to you? To the kingdom?"

Mikalla's body was a massive shadow puppet projected by the light of the many flames and cast onto the wall behind him. A thin smile crept across his face. He licked his lips and fixed his gaze on the official.

"It's belief," Mikalla whispered. The flames seemed to scream and chortle with rage and glee.

"What'd you say?"

"It's belief."

"Speak up, please."

Mikalla, not hesitating for a moment, put both his hands together and configured them in a jumble of fingers and knuckles and a mash-up of palms and nails.

He held out the jumble he'd created with his hands in front of the official's face, as he'd practiced so many times before.

"What is this?" Mikalla asked.

"I'm running out of time," the official sighed. "What is what?"

"*This*!" Mikalla jerked his creation to within an inch of the official's face for him to see and study.

The official sighed again, this time adding the weight of impatience to his brow, as evidenced by the many wrinkles on his frustrated forehead. "I don't know. It's two hands clasped together."

"*No*! Mikalla said. "What are the hands doing? What does it look like to you?"

The official did a facepalm and then looked again at the hands Mikalla held in front of him. "It looks like a mess of fingers."

"Okay, good!" Mikalla got up from his chair and grabbed the candle from the middle of the table.

"W-what are you doing?"

"I'm showing you what the cacao bean is to me."

And then the official finally looked intrigued, gripping his chin in one hand and resting it on another. "Go on."

Keeping his hands in the same mess they were in, Mikalla placed them behind the candle he situated at the edge of the table. Cast onto the wall behind him was a monstrous image. The official's eyes widened. "Now, what do you see?" Mikalla asked.

"Some monster. A crocodile, maybe."

And with that, Mikalla parted his hands again and plucked the cacao bean from the table. He put it in front of the flame up close, so the shadow it projected was a towering mass flickering on the wall—no longer a bean, then a newborn giant.

Mikalla just stared at the official, holding eye contact. "What is this cacao bean now?"

"It's a big shadow."

"Maybe. Maybe it is. But no, not really." The smirk on his face forged itself into a violent smile. "The bean," he looked at it, his voice deepening, "is whatever I want it to be." And he tilted it and contorted it, snapped it, and augmented its image with his rapid fingers shivering on the wall like a great anemone.

The official just sat back with his mouth open. Stiffness pervaded the air. The silence broke the room. The many candle flames yelled and quivered in fear at the hands of Mikalla. Seconds like glaciers oozed by. Mikalla clenched and felt nothing but the tightening of his body back to its stressful default. He squirmed in his chair after his display.

The official furrowed his brow. "Where'd you learn that?"

"Learn what?"

"*That*. Why'd you come up with that?"

Mikalla, tired of the questions, tired of the show, and tired of the official's searing expectations, withdrew into himself. "I don't know."

"What do you mean? Someone must have spoken with you about this. You must be getting told these things."

"I'm not sure. I don't know what you mean."

The official leaned forward and closed his eyes longer than a blink and shorter than sleep. He looked focused, intent on uncovering a precarious layer of Mikalla's mind by prying, picking, crushing it—whatever it took to go deeper into this peculiar student's background. "Mikalla, do you get along with the other kids at school?"

"I think so, yeah."

"Because to me, you seem a little different. You seem—if I may say—special." The official watched with a falcon's eye every twitch in Mikalla's face. And just as the official thought, Mikalla's eyes glowed at the compliment. "Look, you have potential."

"Potential for what?"

"Nothing." The official stood up, wiped his robe off, and turned around. "The time's up. I only wanted to talk to you for a moment. Go and bring the next student in, please."

Nick Oliveri

***

Oh, gods, what are they testing for now? Why me? Why a test? What if I fail? Will my father find out? Maybe my father sent that guy here in the first place. He would never test my brother like this. What is he looking for? What does he even want with me? Do I need to be tested? Oro's thoughts continued to cycle and ravage his mind, washing his rationale away as he wandered the halls, temporarily escaping the threat of the official and the cloud of his weighing anxieties. His steps were short staccatos, miniature stomps in a half-sprint, half-jog to nowhere. His breathing got heavier and quicker, but he did not have the headspace to notice it.

He rambled down a long and lonely hallway, farther and farther away from his classroom, from the official, from the tests, from the expectations, and from the pressure of the teacher. He continued to lumber, and finally, his breathing began to ease. Against a wall, he sighed with his sweaty back.

"Hello there."

Oro jumped. "Ahh! Who's there?" His neck whipped around, scanning for the source of the voice. Only the empty hallway surrounded him. "Show yourself." The voice was not much older than his—boyish but not scared, soft but not timid. From around the corner, a teenager with tattered robes appeared.

"Hi," the teenager said. He held his hand up.

"Who are you?"

"I'm um," Kitan said, looking down at his grubby hands and frayed robes, "I'm nobody."

"Well, that's not true," Oro said. "Everybody's somebody."

"If that's the case, then who are you?"

The boy gulped. "Well, I'm supposed to be...." It would be safer, Oro figured, not to say anything about his royal identity in front of a peasant commoner. Too many bad things could happen, too many sour outcomes for his brain, or his heart, to take. "I'm nobody too."

"Well," Kitan said, his eyes glowing, "since we're both a couple of nobodies, then why are we even here?"

"Where? What do you mean?"

"*Here*. The high noble schoolhouse. A nobody doesn't belong here." Kitan licked his lips delicately with a tongue so snake-like it nearly looked pronged and sharp.

Oro turned away. Away from Kitan, away from his classroom. "Maybe you're right."

"What'd you say?" Kitan stepped closer.

"I *said*, maybe you're right."

"What's your name?"

"Oro. What's yours?"

"Kitan. Just Kitan. Plain Kitan. Two syllables, but infinite power."

Oro scoffed but laughed from his gut. He smiled, showing his teeth and relenting his tough veneer, feeling it melt away at this boy's confidence.

"What's so funny?"

"Well, you're so confident, yet you wear rags."

Then it was Kitan's turn to laugh. Like a hyena, his gut exploded with a howl and a chuckle. But as quickly as he laughed, his face turned serious. "If my *rags* reflected the contents of my mind, they would be beautiful and intricate like yours." He pointed at Oro's fine royal robes. He could see the purple tones in the patterns of the boy's garb, signifying royalty. Kitan was not ignorant.

"Well, mostly anyway," Oro said.

"Why just mostly?" Tilting his head, Kitan slithered like a snake toward prey.

"Well, you wouldn't be allowed to wear purple."

"And why is that?"

"Don't you know?"

"Regardless," said Kitan, waving his hand and looking away, "I feel like you're not a nobody, but maybe you're treated as such."

"Why do you say that?"

"I don't know. Maybe I just feel like you're a pure soul. Maybe I'm wrong. But I feel like you've had it tough." Kitan stared.

"Why are you here again?"

Kitan was only honest, direct, humble, and clear, which was all Oro wanted anyone to be. But it was rare to Oro, rarer even than the gold piled away in his palace. Kitan told him that he was merely a bathroom cleaner and that he'd never been in a building so marvelous before.

Oro said to him that he was a prince, the second in line to the throne, and the son of Menizak III.

Kitan's lips wormed across his face into a slimy, crescent smile. "Why aren't you the first in line?"

Oro felt a shudder like a violent draft roll down his spine. This was a question he'd never been asked—one he'd never asked himself. One he never wanted to. "I have an older brother."

"I wish I had one of those," said Kitan, staring at the ground and then peering toward Oro.

"What? An older brother? *Trust* me. You won't want one of those."

"Well, why not?"

As Oro described all the ways that he was tormented and mangled and emotionally stunted and pushed and beaten by his older brother, Kitan heard the smelting, melding, and shaping of the shiny metallic key to Oro's heart. Every detail was like a fine blade gifted from Oro to Kitan. Every horrendous memory was like a chunk of the boy's tender, still-pulsing heart—in all its ruby flesh.

In the prince's plight, he found a flash of his vision, materialized, crystalline, *real*. He saw in Oro's eyes some kind of way into the future. *Finally, someone who could help me. Finally, a means to make my vision come true.* He saw it all in Oro's pain—an "in," a way forward, a key to the future.

"Well, it's precisely unfair."

"What is?"

The young bathroom cleaner walked on and swept his arm through the air like a racket. "All of it, Oro. All of it is unfair. None of it you deserve. You never asked to be born into a family that resents you."

"Well, I wouldn't say they resent me."

"Yeah, but you can do nothing about it, or at least you *feel* that way. Your brother treats you however he feels; I'd bet you feel powerless to stop it. But, Oro, you can do *so much*. You have freedom beyond your wildest imagination; power is just waiting to be exercised by you."

"Why are you here again?" Oro asked, cutting the raggedy boy off.

Becoming The Conjurer

"I was enlisted into the civil service and orphaned at a young age. I'm here to clean the bathrooms. I am a simple peasant worker."

"Not anymore, you aren't."

Cautious defiance rose within both boys—something of a silent agreement, a truce, a partnership. More words were exchanged—a soft smirk followed. A hand waved. A head nodded. And then they parted ways.

Chapter 5

Mikalla looked out the regal window of the classroom, diverting his eyes from Jani's back. He watched the sun spill its pink glint through the classroom window, signaling the end of the school day. His lungs passed a heavy sigh as his teacher and the rest of the students began to pack up their things. Mikalla followed suit. He sat his burlap satchel on the desk in front and began to put his things away.

His fingers scampered to put everything in its place to go away, far away, from the teacher and the school, the candles in that conference room, and the official that only stared with snake-like eyes. His back tensed and arched. His books and notes were scrawled everywhere with intricate drawings and short poems. *I probably embarrassed myself in that 'test.' Gods, I need to get out of here. One more pointed question aimed at me, and I think I'll spill my guts all over the damn floor. Those eyes of the official.... What did they want with me? What were they trying to find? It's all government nonsense. I hate this goddamn place.*

Most of the students were cleared out by the time Mikalla had all of his things together in his bag and slung over his bony shoulder. The pudgy prince was nowhere to be found in the room. Anywhere in the school building, for that matter. Mikalla took a step toward the door.

Then, the deep screech of Master Chapauhtli's voice cut deep into his spine and rang in between his ears. "Mikalla, stay and see me, please. We need to talk." Mikalla spotted smirks and cringing faces from the other students leaving. He saw Jani's face: flicking thin eyebrows and a dashing smile that seemed to say, "*I'm glad I'm not him.*"

"Yes, Master?"

"Mikalla," he cleared his throat and looked up at the ceiling, seeming to search for an answer or some signal that would never come, "do you know why I'm asking you to stay?"

He shook his head. Lips clasped iron-tight. He found his eyes resting on the floor like anvils. His whole body clenched and shivered.

"No idea at all? Are you sure?"

Mikalla nodded. "Yeah, I think so."

"Well, it's the Official. He said he wants to see you."

A pulse of the sun's energy and intensity exploded in Mikalla's spine. His eyes widened. "Uhm, okay. Is everything okay? Did I fail? Please, sir, I cannot afford to fail out of here, my parents would—"

"*Mikalla.* It's fine. You didn't fail. In fact, I believe you did quite well." The teacher seemed to chuckle. "I don't know what it is, though. He said he'd meet you at the front of the school at sundown. You only have a few moments if you want to be on time."

He lurched for his things and nearly ran to the main entrance of the school. He watched out the window as he ran. He saw the sun bleed from the many cuts that daylight brought. He watched it retreat into its corner, readying itself for another fight, another round with the scourge of day and life and humans and the mountains that provided the backdrop. He saw the official, a statue superimposed and gleaming in the ambitious and oncoming moonlight.

"Hello, sir."

"Mikalla! It's a joy to see you out here. I'm glad you could make it."

Well, I kind of had to. It's not like you leave me a choice. You, the teacher, the state, the school—none of you leave me any choice. I'm here because you want me to be.

"Come, follow me. We have a lot to get to." The official turned around to walk ahead. "Oh, and let me ask you: have you ever been to the city commons? No? Well, it's about time I take you there so you can see for yourself. We have a lot to see. And your parents know you're with me."

**

Mikalla felt the night's wind descend upon him like daggers. "Come. We'll go to the entrance gates. Just stick close to me. Oh, and you can't wear those in the commons—not unless you want to attract a lot of attention." He handed Mikalla an oversized brown cloak. "You're gonna need this."

Why is he taking me here? Why now? Why is it like this?

They passed the guards and descended. The stairs themselves on the way down to the commons grew grittier and more cracked and grayer as they descended lower and then lower yet. Mikalla's sandals were caked with dust. He cringed.

"We've got a little way to go," the official said.

Agitated, Mikalla looked down at his tarnished footwear and asked the reason for doing this in the first place. For some reason or another, he felt entitled to an answer.

They continued to descend. Past bugs and critters and all sorts of birds, past languid hillscapes and serene songs of creatures flying. They continued until a hum and a buzz reverberated through the air, penetrating the muzzle of the nighttime wind. It was a gentle mess of a sound, something soft but building inside the ear. Something that arose and did not cease but only got louder and louder and louder yet.

The buzz of the city was consistent and smooth, like an instrument played by the deft hands of a god. Mikalla had never heard such a noise, such a hum in his ear that only got louder and never wavered—not even for a moment.

"That's the city," the official said, smiling. "This place is what makes the good king's gold shine and his silk smooth. This place is the engine."

"What do you mean by that?" Mikalla asked as the hum of the city commons grew louder and more vibrant.

"You'll see," said the official, still smiling as if he'd invented all of Idaza himself. They walked on and on, down the steps and toward the site of many roofs and the tops of heads like scurrying ants. "So, Mikalla, your parents are clerks, right?"

Poison seeped into Mikalla's gut. *How embarrassing. Especially in front of a high court official.* He cringed. "Yes."

"Very well. And you've never been down here?"

"No. Never."

The steps of both the official and the boy sank into the ground as the dust became clay and the concrete stairs became wooden. A layer of brown caked onto Mikalla's graying sandals and feet. The hum he once heard became a constant bass drum booming in a chorus of giant echoes—rocky pulses, shrill voices, pots clattering about like a horse's frantic hooves. The buzz became a yell, shrill, constant and anxious. The city sprang upon him. At once, the official nearly bounded as his feet hit the ground. "Follow me and stay close. You *have* to stay close." They took off and weaved through people carrying giant pots and old men sitting on the sidewalk.

They continued on past smokers and drinkers and swordsmen and concerned parents yelling for their children to come home for the night. The torches all around were like a clattering constellation of scintillating stars; Mikalla felt like he was running through a cacophonous, smoky dream. The cold wind lashed his face in bursts, but he didn't seem to mind as he ran and shimmied through the bustling markets past monkeys and many children his age playing games that he, too, played with his friends. The spirit of the city was alive and infectious. Every torch a new wonder, and every shop a new world to run past and scan and see all around. People everywhere—Mikalla had never seen so many people at once.

"Here, here, look!" The official said.

"What? I can't hear you!"

"*Look*!" He said it again, and they both stopped. "Hey, and keep your hood on, please. Remember—no attention." Just up ahead was a violent-looking dance by a group of men, muscular and writhing about, playing instruments of all sorts. Some had the instruments up to their mouths, and some had them in hand, shaking and rattling for a hissing noise more perfect and destructive than even a snake's wrath.

The drummers had wide eyes and huge muscles, beating their instruments in a controlled rhythm. Some just danced, and others danced with maracas, and costumes of feathers green and red and yellow and orange adorned the women. It was all violent and beautiful and consuming like a tornado from afar.

But Mikalla wanted to be in the middle of it. His eyes glowed in the torchlight. His mouth dropped and stayed wide open, going dry from the wind.

"This is a street performance," said the official, waving his hand. The music blasted, spit, and kicked in the open air. The people around seemed to become infected by its aura—something about the torches and the blaring instruments shaking the feathers rhythmically, a wave of blushing rainbows across a speckled starlight sky.

Mikalla watched all the people around him become consumed by everyone else. He watched the people dance, and the more they danced, the more others were impelled to join in the madness. And on it went, the full, mad display, glittering in the cascade of torchlight.

"Where are we going?" Mikalla asked.

"Here. This is where we're going."

"What is it?"

"The pulse, Mikalla. It's the heartbeat of the kingdom. The people gathering," he said, having to yell over the music, "are what make this kingdom run. And once you learn what connects them," the official said, "then you can learn how to control them."

Chapter 6

Like all five of her siblings, Jani had long, dark hair and dark eyes to match. As soon as she walked through the front door of her family's castle, her usual cocky smile faded, and her head swiveled around on high alert. An air of fear gripped her neck and chest, tensing her tight shoulders on the balls of her feet. She was the youngest of six children. Feeling like she prey in her own house was not new for her.

She looked for her father, but as a high priest in the kingdom, he was still busy at work long after sundown. She searched for the family dog—something, anything, to distract her from her siblings. Thankfully, she spied her mother in the kitchen, speaking with a servant.

"Jani, hello! There's my baby. How are you?"

"Hi. Good. Have you seen Father?"

"He's still at work—busy with rituals. Could I get you something to eat? We have fresh mango and bananas on the counter."

"I'm okay," Jani said. "I'm not hungry."

And then, like the clouds of a storm, she heard the thundering steps of one of her older brothers. His breathing clapped against the walls, and her ears and mouth soured and cringed. "Okay," said her mother, "they'll be on the counter if you change your mind." She turned toward the thundering noise from the hallway nearby.

"Gobi, is that you? Come give your mother a kiss."

A boy came out from the hallway, not much older than Jani herself. He was tall and thin and wore jewels like a second garment. He had a thin gold and red mask that just wrapped around his eyes, and he carried himself upright with his nose held high. He hugged his mother with long, skeletal arms draped in shining white. It was a quick, haphazard hug, then he got back to holding his nose high and facing toward Jani. "I heard a high court official came to your class looking for recruits," he said in a nasal voice, "and it's a shame you were there."

"Gobi, be nice!"

Jani looked away. "I did well," she mumbled.

Gobi, adorned in royal jewels—some purple and some sparkling sun-white—laughed and replied quickly. "Yeah, I bet," he taunted, "you'll probably wind up with an *amazing* job like being on the school committee or something. Not just because you're the king's cousin or *anything*."

"Gobi, please stop it. Job selection in school is a stressful process. *You* know *that*. Not everyone can be trained to be The Conjurer."

The boy just huffed and smirked and turned away. Jani walked away, too, while her mom stared at her. Rosy, angry redness flushed Jani's java complexion as her walk turned to a run and her hands covered her crying face. She cried because she was hurt. She cried because she knew the truth. She would never be good enough, not then or ever.

How could I be good enough when my brother's going to be The Conjurer and all my other siblings are at the top of their classes, and all they can do is look down on me? They trip me, they beat me, and it's for good reason. Of course, they pick on me—I'm a disgrace. I'm not strong. I'm not as smart as them. I'm not artistic, and I never win any of their games. I'm just the youngest. I'm a baby. I'm just a punching bag, and I deserve it.

As the poison thoughts bled out of Jani's head, so did the tears well in her eyes and run down her face with the force of a mountainous river, flowing, eroding, waving, and rushing right past the hills of her cheeks and the delta of her lips. She cried because that was all she could do. She cried because she knew the truth. She cried because she felt she never should have been born—a mistake among purposeful, perfect people. She was the only one.

"Jani," her mom said and knocked on the door.

"Go away!"

"Come on, just open up. I just want to talk. Are you alright?"

"I'm not fine! I'm not fine, and I never will be! How could I be? How could I be good enough, mother? Tell me!"

"Just open up, Jani."

Silence. Long and drawn out, crushing her mother's caring heart. Silence.

"Jani, don't say that about yourself."

"So what, then? You want me to pretend I'm as good as Gobi?"

"Just open up, Jani. Yes! I do want that. Because it's true, Jani! You *are* as good as Gobi. You're as good as anyone."

***

Gobi, away from his mother and sister, headed back to his room. It was his solace, his office, and his sanctum. Pictures were placed everywhere on his desk and the walls. Etchings of shadows, fires, and dates were scribbled all over them, as were massive crowds admiring a brilliant individual, giant, and looming over them as a colossal silhouette. He drew starry night skies and open horizons, clouds that moved away, and endless oceans.

Parchment covered the walls and even some of the windows. The sunlight that did enter the room made his shiny wardrobe glisten—the only aspect of his room more detailed than his drawings. He walked in and took a deep breath with his eyes closed. He then dashed over to his desk and sat in front of a large piece of amate parchment that covered almost the entire surface. Instead of the usual pictures spread throughout his room, on the big parchment in front of him was a long block of nothing but writing.

Letterings and paragraphs covered the page, scrawled all throughout. It was a story that he looked through all the time. One he cherished with wide eyes and worked on throughout the day. It was the story of a boy growing up; of a boy desiring and striving for actualization and transcendence to the pinnacles of power.

Gobi looked it over and smiled. He cracked his knuckles, then picked up his quill and got to writing furiously. When he was not training to be The Conjurer, this is what he did. This was all he could do. This was all it took to make him happy. Gobi was an artist. He found the rich confines of his mind through writing. He impressed others through performing. He had no competition that he was aware of. He had no bars, no stops, and no roadblocks on the way to his beautiful and glamorous future as the kingdom's Conjurer. He directed everything toward this goal—obsessed, consumed by the flare blitz of the ceremonial flame that shined every week. He worked and worked on the page and then another until the sun began to dip into the hills, submerging the land under the frightful power of the glowering moon. He yawned and smiled a bit at the words he put down—of himself, of his future, of the kingdom itself. Still in his chair, his eyes shut hard under the weight of a nighttime's sleep.

    He tossed and turned in a frenzy of unsettling dreams of disturbances. He saw visions of a newcomer, a dragon or goblin, or maybe just a vicious person cloaked in poor clothes, approaching him and staring. He was skinny and young and handsome, with poor posture and determined eyes set in a poor and stolid face full of nothing but anticipation. Gobi didn't sleep well that night. He didn't like what he saw, and neither water, air, nor meditation could lull him back to sleep. Nothing soothed him that night. And then the sun rose in screaming light. It grated on his eyes. It tore at his face. The power of the morning sun, usually a joy to Gobi, weighed on his restless shoulders.

Nick Oliveri

What the hell is going on? He thought as he got up to get dressed, trying to wipe the sleepy goo from his eyes but failing over and over.

The age of Mikalla was about to set in on his life. With the screaming light of that morning, a new (and more turbulent) chapter was about to begin for the gold-gilded boy.

Chapter 7

"I'm proud of you, son." Mikalla's father beamed at him at the breakfast table. He was a broad man and had a broad smile for Mikalla, who sat across from him, eating his favorite avocado mashup. His mouth was full.

Some deep sense of fulfillment trickled deep into his core. Something whole and good filled him up when he saw his father's smile. He respected his father—not for his career but for his character, his wit, and his integrity. Through a mouthful of avocado and spices, Mikalla said, "Thanks dad," smiled to himself, and kept chewing.

"Do any of the other students know that you got special treatment from the official?"

"Not sure. They knew I got called back after class, but I don't think they knew what we did."

"That's amazing, Mikalla, it really is. I mean, you're being mentored by a high court official to train to have a chance of becoming The Conjurer! It doesn't get any better than that." He beamed. "My son, The Conjurer."

"I'm not The Conjurer's apprentice yet. There's a lot to do. Plus, who knows who else is being trained? There can only be one, you know."

"I know, I know. Just fun to think about." His father smiled again.

And as Mikalla finished chewing, a knock stung the door and boomed throughout the house. It reverberated all around the area and nearly shook the breakfast table where they sat. "I'll get it," said his father. Mikalla furrowed his brow and stood up and looked over toward the entryway, going over all of the ridiculous possibilities of who could be at the other end of that authoritative knock.

Who could that be?

And when his father opened up the door to a short man with a silly hat and frilly clothes, he made a sour face like a skunk sprayed the area. "Hello, sir—can I help you?"

"Good day, indeed. I am here on behalf of The Conjurer himself, Yolia."

Mikalla's father immediately reached for his hand and his shoulders in a primal urge he couldn't contain or hide out of pure excitement. "Wow! You know Yolia, oh, oh, it's a true pleasure, sir. Please, come in and sit down. We have avocados and I could make some coffee for you as well—"

"Actually, I'm here for Mikalla."

"Oh…*oh.*"

Mikalla nearly jumped and headed toward them. "Good morning, sir; it's a pleasure. I'm Mikalla."

"Oh, yes, yes. It's nice to meet you. Yolia, The Conjurer, is *waiting* for you. Gather your things. I will lead you out and to his studio as soon as you're ready. Make it quick—Yolia does not like to wait."

"I'm ready to go *now*." His father looked down at the boy—impetuous and talented and scared of nothing. He wished he could have those years back. He saw a bit of himself in Mikalla—in his fearlessness and quiet confidence, in his determined eyes and sharp jawline.

"Good. Then we will be on our way, then."

"Bye."

"Goodbye Mikalla. Good luck."

***

With every passing step and breath, it seemed like the houses grew. Mikalla's mouth dropped open at the sight of the colossal mansions passing one by one, each one larger than the last. "Have you ever been to this part of the Inner Gardens before?"

"No, but this is amazing." There was a circle of them that all faced a giant statue of a valiant-looking warrior with a spear in hand. The statue depicted

Menizak I, the founder of the kingdom of Idaza. The great one. The mansions got fewer and farther between until they went past the houses and toward the government buildings. The studio came into sight, and as they approached, it towered in front of the eager boy. He felt bubbles of black fear. Red-scorching nerves at the sight of the studio. *The Conjurer is actually in there.*

"Okay," the short man said, "it's right here. I'll escort you in, and then Yolia will take it from there."

And there he was. The Conjurer himself. Yolia in the flesh, in the flashy robes and the headdress like a gentleman's noble hat. He was tall, huge, even. His long bones looked made of iron. His gaze was the opposite, though. His eyes stared long, way in the distance as if adrift in a dream. He looked up, from side to side, and all around. He then fixed his gaze on Mikalla, who had just entered.

"Well, welcome, my boy!"

He towered over the boy and put his large palm on his head.

"You aren't much for engineering and math, are you now, son?" Yolia shook his head and laughed to himself. "Guess that's why they sent you to little old me."

"Sir, I cannot tell you how much of a privilege it is to talk to you. I'm—I'm speechless."

"Well, get less speechless, because you'll have to speak a lot." Yolia turned away from the boy and walked toward his empty stage at the back of the studio, passing through the many seats for the audience. "Come, follow me." And with his back still turned and striding away, he asked the boy, "do you know why you're here, Mikalla?"

"You know my name?"

"Of course I do, Mikalla. Your name's been going around in my circle lately. I guess Tarik was very impressed with you." The Conjurer laughed again to himself.

"Tarik?"

"The official you spoke to—the one that took you downtown. His name is Tarik."

Mikalla saw himself at the precipice of something great and daunting and dangerous, the ledge before a pit of monsters, a trial and a triumph. *I have a lot to learn,* he thought to himself.

Yolia asked again, "so Mikalla," he said, "do you *know* why you're here? Why am I taking the time to do this? To talk to you? After all, I *am* the big, bad Conjurer. I could be working on the next ceremony's performance. But I'm with you right now. Right here. *Why*? Do you know?"

"Honestly, I don't know, sir."

"Please, just call me Yolia."

"I don't know, Yolia."

He faced Mikalla then, not moving or shifting his focus anywhere. Mikalla saw The Conjurer's hands clench and fingers rub against one another, twitching with force and stress. "I called you in personally after hearing the official talk about you. He said you put on quite the show in that conference room. And Mikalla," he bent down to get closer to the boy's face, squinting and smiling, "putting on shows is what I do."

Mikalla felt a surge of something devouring his chest, his insides aching from excitement, and his head not quite believing that this was all real. But it was. And eventually, he figured that his prayers were paying off, that his inner visions of his own future began to hold weight, and that his dreams of becoming The Conjurer could actually crystallize at some point.

But right as Yolia said that, a sound came from the studio's entrance. Both Yolia and Mikalla turned to face the ruckus. It sounded like someone banged on a brick with a wooden mallet. "Come in!" Yolia said.

And then a burst of energy filled the room. Purple and gold radiated through the doorway, and then a face appeared through the sunlight. *He's wearing purple? He must be a royal,* Mikalla thought. But Mikalla didn't recognize the face. Mikalla didn't recognize anyone like this.

"Gobi," The Conjurer said, "come this way." He was older than Mikalla, only by a few years, but had a boyish look to him, like he'd never been challenged and had never aged by a single thing.

Gobi entered the room smiling, but soon had his toothy grin wiped clean off his face when he saw Mikalla. He approached with tight knees, tight steps, and tightly squinted eyes. His voice was high but strong and scratched. "Who is this? Who is this boy in my seat?"

"Gobi, calm down. There's a seat right over there. This boy is here to help you train. He's talented." The Conjurer with white teeth of furious sun smiled. "One could say, *special*, even—special enough to be working with us."

Gobi walked over to his seat. He never took his eyes off Mikalla. At Yolia's words, Mikalla felt his heart sink. *So, I can't be The Conjurer? Is this just a ploy? I may be a pawn.*

Yolia had one of his great legs crossed over another. "Gobi, calm down. Please. Take a breath. It's all good, okay?"

Gobi huffed. Finally taking his eyes off Mikalla, he looked down at his own new leather sandals, which shone in the natural light of the cavernous studio. "What do we have in store today?" Gobi asked.

"Oh, we have a lot to do and all the time to do it. I'm kidnapping you guys, and we're taking a trip to the commons."

"Another one?" Gobi said.

"This will be a special one. We won't waste any time either. Grab the overcoats by the door each. We'll head out right now."

***

And so they ventured down to the gates and then down further. Past the guards. Past the steps. And past the gates further, below the Inner Gardens and into a lower land, a louder place filled with people and dirt and opinions. Mikalla heard the yelling and the open-air trade bellowing through the streets and bouncing off the terra cotta walls and roofs of the city. Mikalla recognized the crowds, but this time it was different. This time, he got to see the commons in the open air during the daytime, a place of business that pumped the blood of the economy. No ceremonies were being performed.

There was no dancing. No singing. No instruments nor flashy feathers worn. Strictly, Mikalla saw people walking vigorously to and fro, sometimes yelling and sometimes keeping their heads down as they passed a crowd with a pot or a chicken in hand.

"Where are we going?" Gobi asked.

"Just up ahead. It's at the end of the market."

"A shop?"

"Kind of."

And the crowd thinned a bit as they approached the end of the massive bazaar, getting quieter and softer with distance. Yolia pointed to a small and shabby hut. "This way." And The Conjurer, cloaked in plain and cheap brown cloth, led them into a tented hut where they had to crouch to enter.

An old man stood at the counter. "Buy?" He asked with a straight stone face, eager, boyish eyes set in old, leathery skin.

"Yes, but we want to browse first."

At that, the old man yelled something to the back of the store. His voice was quick and gruff. There was an entrance somewhere behind him where his voice carried. Tinkering could be heard from behind him.

"Can we go back there?" Yolia asked the old man.

The man's eyes lit up. "Yes! Yes, sure, sure!" Then, to the backroom: "Wendi, we have buyers coming in the back!"

The three walked in the back room and had to duck yet again under the tented entryway to where Wendi the pot maker sat criss-cross on a shag carpet with half of a wet pot in front of her. It sat on a pedestal that seemed to rest on some wheel on the ground.

"Oh, a potter," Gobi said, "wow! Look at all these." They walked around as Wendi eyed them. On shelves and counters all around were pots and clay containers of all sorts of shapes and angles. Mikalla couldn't help but stare at Wendi, the potter. She looked back.

She had sad eyes. But deep within, somewhere in the pitch black of her pupils, was a glint of hope, of joy, of life, and of vitality. She had a sunken brow on top of a weathered and worn face. Her hair was dark but graying. It looked like pepper and powder had been sprinkled throughout her head and face. She wore a tentative frown. *But those eyes,* Mikalla thought, *they say something I can't grasp. I don't know what it is about those eyes….*

Yolia turned to the boys. "See why we came now?"

Gobi nodded his head. Vigor dripped from his words. "This is great. This is amazing. Look at all these!"

Yolia then turned to Mikalla. "What do *you* think, Mikalla?"

Gobi turned toward him too. He wore a look of disgust, like Mikalla was some malicious bug. Something corrosive and untouchable. Mikalla, because of that look from Gobi, still felt out of place. Where he belonged, he didn't know. He felt even lower than the potter, who sat on the ground before him with sad eyes. "It's cool," Mikalla said. "It's uhh… there are so many variants." Then Mikalla tried to snap out of his spell. He asked Wendi, "are these all made by you?"

"Yes," she said. And she waved her hand at the array on the shelves, some on the floor, some hoisted on counters.

Yolia looked back at Wendi. A smile crawled across his face, opening up like a flower blooming. "And Wendi, if I may ask—because we're so impressed, and we *will* buy—why do you do this?"

Wendi, still sitting, looked puzzled. "What do you mean?"

Mikalla was just as confused as Wendi. Gobi just stared at Yolia, mirroring his every move. "I mean, why do you do this? Why is it that you come here every day and make these pots? Your hands get cut and sore, your body aches, and you get hungry, presumably. But you still do it. Every day. All these wonderful pots. Why do you do it?"

Wendi looked all around, gulped, and then stood up from her criss-crossed position. She was short and squat, and she wore a long, plain garment. She squinted at Yolia. She wasn't angry, but rather stern and determined. Standing up, she said without any hesitation, "because I have to."

Because I have to. Because I have to. The words rang in Mikalla's head. It made him feel dizzy inside. *Because I have to. Why else? Why else would anyone do anything?*

Yolia looked like a child—giddy, nearly jumping at Wendi's response. But he kept his composure. "That's amazing. We'll buy three. Take your pick, boys."

What were the pots to him? What were the pots to her? Why did Yolia choose this place? *Why did he take us here?*

Mikalla continued to look around after Gobi quickly chose a pot. Gobi put it up to Yolia, as if to have his teacher inspect and approve his choice. The pot Gobi chose had a certain sheen to it. It had stripes and intricate carvings of the battles, which Yolia himself told stories of. It had etchings of great warriors—hand carved by Wendi, of course.

"Did you make these pictures?" Yolia said to Wendi. Despite her standing, he still looked down on her from the top of his huge frame.

All Wendi did was nod and say yes.

"It's beautiful," Yolia smiled, "they're beautiful," he said, pointing to the warriors and the small people at the other end of their spears, all engraved in the clay with a shining finish. It was a labyrinth of colorful scenes of the strongest kind—blood spilling, couples mating, the sun shining on rain-soaked trees after a violent storm. It was all there, and Yolia was clearly impressed, definitely with Wendi's creation, and maybe with Gobi's choice.

Becoming The Conjurer

But Mikalla continued to just look around. He browsed and browsed. This was something he'd never done. Going shopping for pots. Staring at mounds of clay, lifeless but somehow alive and breathing, too. Immobile, but somehow pulsing with life. He wore spectacles of sad, contemplative eyes. He then turned to Wendi. "Who are you?" Mikalla asked the woman, who then looked at the boy in brown. She furrowed her brow.

"What d'you mean?"

"Who are you? What's your identity?" Mikalla said.

"I'm Wendi. Who are *you*?" Her face one time flicked with anger and then receded back into confusion.

"My name's Mikalla. But I'm not really sure who I am yet."

The woman looked frustrated. "Okay," she said flippantly. "Find any pots you like?"

"But I know who you are if you made these pots," Mikalla said, scanning the room with clouds in his eyes, "I know who you are. I can tell by your handprint and toil, by the very stripes you carved with sore fingers and red wrists. I can tell. I know you by your work." And then Mikalla walked around some more. Then all eyes were on him—Yolia, Gobi, Wendi, the whole lot. "And your work," the boy said through a whisper, "is beautiful."

Wendi immediately started crying and hugged the boy.

Chapter 8

"So how many times have you been to the commons?"

"Hmm. Maybe a couple."

"And you're the prince? And you've only been to the city a couple times?"

"Well, I live in the city."

"Not my part of the city," Kitan said, half smiling at his new, naive friend. "What do you think?"

"It's different," Oro said. They were sitting on top of a building under a spray of stars and nighttime blackness, the gleam of the moon hitting off the many roofs and torchlights that dotted the cityscape.

"Well, you're the prince; shouldn't you be experiencing war and markets and work and what so many of your people do everyday? Shouldn't you understand their struggles as a ruler?"

"You should," Oro said. And then he sighed and looked down. "But I'm not going to be a ruler. I'm not going to be much of anything. I'm just a prince not destined for whatever—not a craftsman, not a warrior, and *certainly* not a king."

Kitan had the look of a wolf upon desperate, helpless prey. "You matter," he said. "You matter, and you don't even know it. Your brother doesn't have to say you matter. You matter for yourself. You matter to… me." Kitan looked down at his dangling legs. "I've never had a friend, really. I just work and work—never had much of a family either. But I know I matter. The visions in my head matter."

"Visions? What do you mean?"

"I see mistakes. I see them everywhere. And I see how they could be fixed. It wouldn't take much to make them better."

"That's kind of cool."

"Not cool to me." Kitan sighed, "without being able to do a thing about it. It's agonizing. All of it."

Throughout the conversation, Oro only heard bits of himself in Kitan's words. Images of his hurt and how Kitan was trapped, so was Oro. Somehow, they were aligned. Kitan was trapped, much like Oro himself. Oro could feel Kitan yearn for something better, something grander. The young prince had not the slightest clue quite what Kitan yearned for specifically, but they still shared the same type of desire. He shared the pain, unlike what most of his noble peers felt. Oro was encumbered by everyone in his life. He was a prince in a palace or a prisoner in a golden cage. The more questions he asked

Kitan, the more it seemed like they fit together, like they could somehow help each other.

"You seem to be pretty good with people," Oro blurted out after some time. "Managing them, going in between them and around them."

"What do you mean?"

"Well, for one, you met me. You just seem to be in the right place at all the right times. I don't really know anything beyond that. Anyways, there are a lot of treacherous people in my life, and I feel like you could help me."

Kitan smiled a wolfish smile behind his back. His teeth flashed like sunlit fangs in the night air. "Well, I have a vision for this nation," Kitan said, "and I think you could help me too."

Oro stood up. And however short and stout he was as a boy, he grew colossal in that instant. He towered over Kitan and the rest of the city, commons, Inner Gardens and all. He was the prince in silk, and his eyes shone with razor fear and focus. He held out his limp and mighty hand with his palm facing down. "I want you to be my royal adviser. Every royal has the right to any adviser they choose. I want you to be mine. You're an outsider. I need that."

The night wind gripped and chilled them both, and it shook the city below them. Kitan kneeled before the prince while he hid his eyes, yellowing from sick ambition and silver dreams manifested. He took Oro's hand and lightly kissed it, as was customary for a subordinate. Although he kneeled right then, Kitan was on his way up.

"I promise to protect you, my prince."

"And I promise to keep your identity secret. From now on, you will be my royal adviser. As long as you stick by me, no longer will you be a street sweeper that hides away in the dirt."

***

Meanwhile, on the frontier, King Menizak had his own war tent, lit by torches, and he spoke with his son inside. Outside, countless tents littered the valley as the Idazan military rested in a war camp for the night.

"This'll be easy," Menizak IV said, his youthful voice filled with vigor despite the late, quiet night.

"Son," his father said, "they may be savages, unorganized, and untamed, but that should have no bearing on your attitude. We treat every conflict the absolute same. We treat every battle the same. And son," the king paused for a second and frowned, furrowing his brow, "battles are *never* easy."

Prince Menizak just bowed and looked toward the ground. "Understood, father. Of course."

"Hey," the king said. The ice in his stern look melted away. "Get up." And Menizak the older stepped toward the prince, and, although night lurked everywhere and all around them, they were insulated by the light of the tent. "I love you, son."

"I love you too, father."

Chapter 9

It was just Gobi and Yolia in The Conjurer's mansion. They were each enjoying a drink of rich cacao. The beverage was a rarity throughout the kingdom but a norm for the elite. Whenever Gobi had it, though, his nervous system tensed like a wire pulled from end to end. His jaw always clenched under the influence of the spicy, thick cacao drink, speeding up his already lightning-quick nerves.

The Conjurer yawned, still draped in his morning robe. "So what did you learn from yesterday?"

Gobi nearly jumped. But instead of jumping, he stayed planted like a stone, sinking into his padded chair. He cringed. Yolia just looked. "I'm still discerning it."

"Discerning what?"

"The lesson."

"And why is that?"

"I'm just—it's nothing, really."

"You seem to be disturbed, though, Gobi. Maybe it is something."

"Nope."

"You can tell me."

Becoming The Conjurer

"There's nothing to say," Gobi said. His head shook, a tremor swept down his body quietly, smoothly. A volcano of angst behind his eyes, waiting, wanting, and yearning to erupt.

And then, turning away from Gobi, The Conjurer stood up. His robe flowed like a towering apparition. "Yes, there is, Gobi." Yolia turned the room to ice with the stone of his voice—a stoic, rolling boulder barreling right toward the boy. "We've been through this before. We've been working together for too long." Like a hot knife, the angsty volcano within Gobi bubbled and gurgled. Yolia felt the pain and the anger from the boy, who was too young to be a master, but almost too old to be a mere pupil. Gobi was an apprentice—transitioning, growing, and delving into the great burden of mastery. Yolia understood the pain that Gobi had to go through to reach his position. He was going to make sure he felt the heat. He was going to make sure he could handle it. "Tell me. Tell me, please."

And then, like a red explosion of life and destruction, Gobi blurted out what he was really feeling. "It's—it's Mikalla. Why is he here with us? What is he doing? Is there a reason? I mean, I just don't get it. His presence.... It disturbs me."

Hidden from Gobi was a certain exhilaration, a certain wicked flick of Yolia's bushy brow, some tampering stroke in his face. Yolia smiled. "Why do you think that is? That he disturbs you so much?

"I—I wouldn't say he disturbs me that much...."

"Don't lie to me."

"I really don't know, master. I think I'm just scared." Gobi scrunched up, his knees to his head and his elbows to his knees. He shrank like a prune under the phantom of Yolia's shadow. "Scared of what could happen. Scared of a disruption to our routine."

"There are a lot of things to be scared of," Yolia said, his voice still booming over Gobi's scared squeak. "Are you maybe scared for your *job*?"

And then something piqued in Gobi like a violent lightning storm. Quivering and lashing, his tongue connected with his teeth, which gnashed as he stood up and stormed toward the corner of the room, facing away from Yolia then. "No, no, no, that's, that's not true. I'm not. How could I be? I'm your apprentice. You chose me. You chose me because I'm the best. I'm meant for this role, and I've been groomed for years. Of course I'm not scared to lose my job. That's crazy." And then he inhaled shakily. Still, he went on and said, "do I have a reason to be scared?"

"No." Yolia laughed deeply. "You're still my apprentice, Gobi, and you can be sure of that. "There's nothing to be scared of…unless—"

"*Unless?*"

"Unless you mess up royally."

Seared and simmering through Gobi's head were acts of violence, crazed nightmares, and frantic thoughts pulsing every which way.

***

Yolia and the king sat in a cellar in the royal palace. Shelves of bottles and wooden barrels were strewn throughout the rocky room, and they sat across from one another. "So, Yolia, how is Gobi doing?"

The Conjurer smacked his tongue against the roof of his mouth. "Gobi is…being himself. Bold and somehow hesitant. Slow and somehow decisive. It's hard for me to put my finger on him."

The king looked at him strangely.

"*But*, that's why I love him. That's why I love working with Gobi. He's a true artist, and he has a lion's appetite. He's a lot of fun."

"Good," Menizak said. "Very good." I'd presume you're treating my nephew well, but also finding ways to challenge him, to make him a man." The king looked toward the dingy ceiling as he said this, like it was a starry sky. *To make him a man.*

"Well, of course. He is being pushed to his limits. No doubt about that." Yolia had his hands clasped on the thick slab of oak which acted as the table.

"Well," the king started, "I wanted to talk about just *how* he was being pushed. After all, he is my nephew. Therefore, I should have *some* say in how he's trained."

"Not traditionally, but okay."

"What'd you say?"

"Nothing."

"Hmm." Menizak III looked directly at Yolia. He wore a crown of blue and green feathers spanning a universe of splendor. His head, his dress, his skirt, his cape, all were immaculate and thick and bedazzled with shells and stones from the very farthest extent of their known world. His intent eyes were the only dark part of his outfit, and they bore directly into Yolia's spirit. "Anyways, I wanted to talk about the new kid. Mikowel."

"It's *Mikalla*."

"Okay. Well, I wanted to talk about him."

"Alright, and what is that?"

"Why is he there?"

"Like, with me? As in, why is he a part of Gobi's training?" Yolia asked.

"Yes. Exactly that. Why bring this boy into the middle of your process now? At such a dire time of transition. Why now?"

Yolia looked away from the king. The Conjurer hid his face in the shadows, away from the grip of the king's gaze. "Oh, your highness, he's only a helper. I think you've misunderstood my process. He's only there to aid Gobi in replacing me. That is all."

"And how is he aiding you? In what ways do you need this boy instead of just the way it was?"

Still looking away, Yolia's voice softened, but his resolve strengthened. A surge went through him. "Would you like me to challenge Gobi or not?"

The king gave a great pause. His jaw went hard. His fists went hard. A tension like steam wafted between them, around them, filling their noses and choking the tops of their lungs. The king took a sip of water. "I want you," the king said, "to challenge Gobi."

"Then, your highness, where is the problem in my process?"

"In that The Conjurer's apprenticeship should be intimate, special, sacred. This is unprecedented—I mean, a *helper*?"

Yolia felt the weight of the air press against his shoulders. He didn't breathe. "What's unprecedented, your highness, is anyone else getting involved in this process."

"Gobi's my nephew."

"And he's *my* apprentice."

"Why is Mikalla there? Why him over anyone else, if you really need anyone else there?"

"He's talented. He pushes Gobi, even if he doesn't realize it."

The king nodded.

Yolia spoke again. "And I know your nephew can handle that."

"Very well," the king said. That was the last thing he said before motioning for Yolia to follow him back upstairs to the better-lit areas of the wide halls of the royal palace. The Conjurer followed Menizak from a distance and then went his own way after saying his goodbyes and bowing to His Highness.

Chapter 10

"Your father's not going to be happy about this." Kitan heard Oro's mother, and her words were like shrapnel from a knife. Cutting into his chest. Burrowing into his ears. Embedding into his psyche. *Your father's not going to be happy about this. Your father's not going to be happy about this.*

"What do you mean?" Oro was obstinate.

I'm going to get to see the inner workings of power, Kitan thought. It was all happening so quickly, so fluidly, like he was in a dream or trance that lasted days without end. "This is my own personal adviser, Kitan. Any royal can do this, even a young prince."

"It's true, but anything your father says goes." And then Kitan felt some urge or something else tug at him, demanding action. It started in his gut then traveled up to his mouth, where it surfaced for the two others in the room.

"My divine queen," Kitan spoke up and bent down on one knee. He had an arm crossed over his bony chest and bent his head so he could stare at the marble floor. "My name is Kitan, and I was born only to serve.

The health and wellness of your family is all that concerns me."

The queen smiled for a second and then returned to a stoic face. She squinted at the teenager in plain clothes and raggedy hair. She lowered her sneering gaze down at the boy. The queen turned her head, as if trying to figure something out, trying to uncover and fit together the endless puzzle of Kitan. Kitan, the mystic, the plain teen, the subservient rogue. "Yes," she said, and then leaned forward even closer to the kneeling boy, "but why *you*? Why you, specifically?"

"Well, I'm—"

"Ah! Don't answer," the queen said. "You may stop kneeling now. Oro, retreat to your quarters, please. You may bring Kitan with you until sundown, and then he has to go back to…. wherever he *goes*." She said the last part with disgust, like Kitan was a worm instead of a person.

***

The golden glamor of Idaza was built on the premise of bloodshed and destruction. It was the warriors, not the scholars or priests, who ultimately were celebrated, proselytized and immortalized.

Arrows flew like snowflakes glistening in the sun. On their tips, countless tiny daggers glimmered,

Becoming The Conjurer

meant only for the ripping and piercing of flesh. Bodies dropped like rags. Necks ran with crimson rivers on the battlefield. A scuttle of infinite struggling bodies. Many painted with dirt, writhing in the dust. Primal, spittling screams of war ended with gasps as arrows stuck and clung like elegant daggers in the muscular bodies of dying warriors. Their lives left them as quickly as they left their families for war. As soon as enough blood escaped their worming corpses, they became litter. No longer human, just a pile of fleshy rags, red with frying blood. Ankles twisted and popped. Collarbones shattered like brittle wood under the stress of a swinging enemy club.

  A boy with proud feathers entered the battlefield yelling. He was an Idazan warrior, wrapped up in his ego and the traditional costume of an Idazan warrior. He yelled, charging forward with a ringed club in hand and a painted face like a mountain lion. He had the ferocity of a screaming god of death and only death, focusing all his body's wisdom and all his mind's learning on dragging his enemy to the pit of hell and burying him in his own blood.

  An image of his parents flashed in his mind. He thought of how proud they would be if they could only see him now—a charging and painted force of bravery representing his valiant king and beautiful nation. A true warrior, fearless. But his youthful fearlessness was only rewarded with a dull clunk sound as one of the many flying arrows entered his chest. His eyes went from fierce to pale and lifeless. His mouth went from spit-filled and loud to a quiet, gurgling bath of blood. His parents flashed through his dying mind again. He saw their faces. He felt their hugs, their caring embrace. If only he could be back there, in the arms of his mother within the safety of Idaza now.

But instead, he became a pile of pale bones on the dusty surface of war. War. War, the goddess of all things evil and triumphant. The bleeding, screeching devils leered up at him, clambering over one another to drag him down. War, war. It will swallow all.

The Menizaks, both father and son, charged onward. They had no time to mourn the rapid deaths of their own people. They had enemies to take down. They had people to smite. They had families to ruin and prisoners to take. They yelled, swinging and sprinting quickly. Their harsh cries pierced even the sky above.

They charged on and on. They made it to the center of the battlefield, where most of the skirmishes were taking place. Wood splintered like rain all around them. Blood sprayed and ran rivers. Feet and limbs entangled in a web all around them. Menizak IV spotted an enemy who turned around. He then thrust his spear into his back. The victim yelped and hit the ground, dying rapidly as life left his eyes. With his father watching, Menizak the younger took a moment to wrestle his spear from the body that lay on the other end. But then, from the corner of his eye, another enemy came charging at Menizak the younger. His father stepped in front of the screeching maniac and lunged forward with his own pike. A direct shot in the chest. The savage was sent back with force and fell to the ground along with the other enemy. Almost in unison, both father and son wrenched their spears from their enemies and readied again, back-to-back, as they'd done so many times before. And the savages continued to come, stuck in a frenzied parade of sprinting and screeching, their eyes darkened with murder—each time getting closer to the pair of royals who stood in the middle of the whole battle, lunging and spearing and stabbing their way through the thick of the crowd. Each time they triumphed, they came away with a thicker grunt, a harder resolve, and a tighter fury for battle.

One savage snuck behind the lunging prince, who stabbed one enemy. The prince focused on what was ahead. He kept glaring and shaking and dodging. The skill at such a young age resembled a graceful warrior dance, but with life on the line of the choreographed dips and lunges. The savage came forward and swung a spear within an inch of the prince's achilles. The prince paid it no mind, as he was locked in a skirmish with another enemy. The savage behind him struck again, this time connecting with the heel of the prince, sending him flying to the ground. The king saw this and at once neutralized the savage, sending him down the hill with a wild blow.

The king ran over and stood in front of his son. He began fighting rampantly like an angry bull, able to see nothing but red, red, red. Rivers and streams of it. Splotches of it. The goliath king painted the battlefield red with rage and blood as he protected his son. But he began breathing heavily and slowing his swings down, until he had to call in for backup to lift his son and retreat.

"I'm fine, father, I can walk!"

"Nonsense! I'm carrying you."

And as they retreated, the savages looked on and only got angrier and more determined to sack the royals.

Arrows fell like rain. All around them they poured. The King watched as bodies dropped and stumbled and fell. But the brave and big Idazans pushed on as the king carried his son back to the tents. Blood spurted from the wound but proved to be manageable all the same.

They were in the medic's tent. And then the guard at the front grunted in agony. The king reached for his spear as the medic, with scared eyes, looked on and then continued to clean and bandage the prince's heel. The king charged outside of the tent, sweeping his head

Becoming The Conjurer

frantically from side to side. He walked forward and then out of sight.

A silence emerged like a zombie walking, stepping out of the grave. Silence. The prince winced as his deep wound was pressed tightly by the medic with a shaking hand. He swallowed. The medic gulped. They could both hear the dust sweep around in the whims of the wind. They could hear their own breathing. They could no longer hear the king.

And then footsteps crunched the dirt around them. They gingerly hopped. "Hello?" The prince searched for a sign of safety, but nothing came. And then the footsteps froze. All was quiet again. All was still. The prince lay on the table in agony. The medic, in the wake of utter silence, reached for a spear.

But it was too late.

As soon as the medic took his eyes off the door, a savage charged in and piked the medic once in the chest and then again in the head as he fell to the ground. The prince squirmed and lunged for the medic's dropped spear. He felt no pain.

There was no sign of his father. Only the savage and the prince were in the medic's tent—an intimate battlefield. But the tent was too small. The savage was too quick. The savage struck paralyzing fear into the heart of the injured prince. He also drove his spear into his heart. Life left the prince rapidly. The savage struck again. He seemed to know how important the prince was. He seemed to understand the severity of each strike. The savage stared and smiled with an animal twitch of glee at the royal blood pouring onto the ground. And then Menizak III charged in, yelling and striking the savage down. Feathers and blood, quiet wind whispering.

The King looked at the savage first, who lay in a pile, dying. Then he turned his frantic gaze toward his son, who lay on the ground next to the savage. The prince writhed desperately, fighting for the life that he had just moments ago. The king could only stand and stare. He bent down and, with wide eyes, asked his son, "what happened? He's gone now. He's gone. Where's the medic?" And then he spotted the medic too, also lying in blood. A battle scene in a place of healing. That was the way of the savages. The king put bandages and spices and water and all sorts of things on the holes in the prince's chest. Menizak III took the medic and shook his lifeless body off the ground. "What should I do? *What should I do?*" The king yelled.

The dying medic just coughed. The King yelled some more and then called desperately for a transport caravan back to the royal palace.

***

Becoming The Conjurer

They arrived in the grand entryway. The grand entrance was littered with medics and supplies and priests and officials and other nobles.

"Get back! Get back!" the king yelled. "I need the medics! Where are the medics? Anyone who's not a medic or a priest, get out!" And then, in a quieter voice, Menizak III whispered to his son, "you're going to be okay. You're gonna make it—you're a Menizak. Of course you're going to make it. Hey, hey, hey, stay with me."

And then the medics crowded the bleeding body as the prince coughed quietly. The queen just sat and cried, unable to do anything but sit, hunched over with her face in her quivering hands. Sobs followed the profound silence, and then silence fell again, punctuated by sniveling breaths.

The king pressed and ran his hands over his face, much like the dried blood that once ran over the prince's. He breathed heavily. Tears streamed out his eyes, and no matter how much he yelled at the medics and asked them to help, no matter how much he willed and wished and prayed for his son's eyes to fill up with life, only darkness clouded them. The windows to the prince's soul looked bleak.

Oro was alone in the halls of the palace, wandering and daydreaming as he often did, when he heard the yells and the horrid, animalistic cries of his

parents. The hairs on his neck shot up. His breathing stopped for a minute. He crept toward the grand entrance, dreading he ever did so as he saw the unspeakable. poured
His brother's chest gushed blood. Oro froze. He stood lifeless as he watched his brother lie on the marble floor. Standing about forty paces away from Prince Menizak was the closest he'd ever been to death to that point.

Oro continued to stare for an hour. Two hours. Three hours. The day slowly froze into nighttime. The shamans and priests and medics vacated the palace. One by one, they left, and eventually, only his father could be seen with the body. The king laid down next to the prince. The king's silk linens were painted a deep crimson color with the blood of his son. And still, Oro just watched. He watched his father sob, his mother scream toward the heavens, and he watched the life leave his brother, filling the palace with a spirit of unholy deprivation.

It may have been the end for the prince, but it was a new beginning for the kingdom. The era of Oro had begun, and it started with the tepid tears of his frozen father.

Chapter 11

Mikalla awoke to a crashing noise. Glass shattered like a firework, some of which got on his bed, as the rest dispersed on the floor like a great quake of sparkling dust. "Ahh! Who's there? Hello?" At this point, Mikalla kneeled on his bed and put the covers up to his chest like a scared lamb, crouched and searching for an answer. That answer came in the form of a rock on the ground, splayed among the broken glass that lay all around. Mikalla was careful not to step on the glass with his bare feet as he lifted himself out of the bed and stepped toward the rock. He inspected it up close. Nothing extraordinary. He searched for someone or something out the now-broken window that could give a clue. But he found no one.

When he told his parents, they were appalled, but all they could do was say that they would go to an official with the "terrible news."

"But what if I'm being hunted? What if someone's jealous?" Mikalla asked.

"We'll try to find that out when we go to an official. But Mikalla, you're just an assistant, remember?

I don't think anyone—no matter how awesome it is that you're with The Conjurer all the time—is jealous of an assistant. If anything, it'd be that kid, Gobi, that they'd be mad at. Nephew of the king, next in line to be The Conjurer—now *that's* someone to be jealous of.

***

Mikalla walked into The Conjurer's studio and saw both Yolia and Gobi sitting on the stage. "Come, sit," Yolia said, motioning Mikalla over. "Today, we're staying in the studio as part of Gobi's training." Gobi just sat and glared at Mikalla, and—as Mikalla could see out of the corner of his eye—his nostrils flared in some kind of primal disgust. The boy shivered as he sat down.

The studio sounded like a desolate tundra—deadened, cold, and deathly quiet. All was still for a while, as Yolia took his time to take a deep breath and get on with his lesson. *What is this*? Thought Mikalla.

"Today, we're going to be telling stories."

"What kinds of stories?" Gobi asked. It was in the question in Mikalla's head too, but he was too shy, too shaken from that morning, to ask it.

"Stories that *work*,' Yolia said. "Stories that move people."

Becoming The Conjurer

And the lesson continued as Yolia stood up and started pacing. The boys just sat right there. "What is a story?" Yolia asked with his back turned to the boys.

Gobi's voice shot through the silent air like an arrow. "A telling of something that happens. In a story," he continued, snidely and with his eyes closed, "a conflict is necessary, and characters are necessary. Those are what make up the plot—characters maneuvering and doing things, coming into conflict, and then resolving it."

"Wrong."

Gobi looked hurt at the rejection of his answer.

"Mikalla, any guesses?"

Mikalla just shook his head.

"You don't know what a story is?" Yolia smiled to himself.

"Well—"

"It doesn't matter," Yolia cut him off. "A story is a life. It has a life of its own. It's a baby. It's helpless." Yolia continued to pace. His face looked inquisitive. He went on and on and nearly paralyzed both boys with interest. He then stopped pacing and faced them. "And we need people to care about our baby. For our baby to live, people need to care."

The words rang in Mikalla's head. *A story is a life. A story is a baby. For our baby to live, we need people to care.*

Mikalla blurted out words that begged to get out of his head. "How do we make people care?"

But instead of Yolia responding, it was Gobi who spoke next. "Don't talk when The Conjurer is talking, peasant."

"Enough, Gobi." Yolia still smiled, if only slightly more intensely. "That's a good question, Mikalla. That's also the question of the day."

Mikalla looked to the side and saw Gobi glare at him. *Peasant. Is that what I am?* Mikalla thought. He felt deflated and even more out of place. "I need to use the restroom. Where is it?"

"Over there," said Yolia. His smile wore off.

In the bathroom, Mikalla looked at himself. He didn't have to go except to escape from the lesson, from Yolia, from expectations, from rocks thrown, from society, *from Gobi. How could someone so close to power be so trapped*? Yet, that's what Mikalla was—trapped. Hopelessly caged in as a pawn.

He looked in the mirror and saw a ghost. A boy unsure of what to do or where to go. A man on the precipice. A child afraid to grow or stay small. He saw a force in the universe battered around at all his own expense and at none of his own will. He saw in that mirror an animal, full of fear, emptied of resolve, a shell. Someone struggling for some meaning, a reason for the suffering, day in and day out. He saw someone who was unwilling but all too capable. A peasant. *A peasant*—too rich for the commoners and far too poor to be a true noble. Artistically suppressed, creatively deprived, a ghost.

In the dusty mirror, he looked at his own eyes. He saw a boy, a peasant. *A peasant*. Was that all he'd be?

Floating across the obsidian canvas, the ghost watched himself watch himself. *Peasant. A peasant walks here. If a peasant can never be good enough, then why be anyone else but myself?* And then, through watching and thinking, the ghost empowered himself. The phantom peasant, the boy on the precipice, let go of the harshness he inflicted on himself and chose to walk on—out of the bathroom, down the hall, and back to his seat next to Gobi.

Let there be war.

And a war did ensue.

"Mikalla, how was your visit to the bathroom? Did you make it alright?" There was a hint of mockery in Yolia's voice, something ironic but disguised expertly. His words were veiled in something indistinguishable, a cloud.

"Yes sir."

"Very well," Yolia said. "Oh, and call me Yolia, please. None of this "sir"' stuff. Enough with that."

"Yes, Yolia."

"Okay then. Well, Mikalla, as I told Gobi, we're going to be telling stories today. You won't be participating," Yolia said as Mikalla's heart sank, "but rather, you will be judging."

"Okay," said Mikalla. Gobi continued to stare at him, only this time more reserved, this time quieter, in his own way. "Just let me know what I need to do."

"I'll tell you," he said, pacing with his back turned away from the boys once again. "Gobi is going to start. He's going to tell us a story, or, in the way I described it, present his very own baby to us. I want you to judge it based on how much he made you *care*."

Mikalla's heart swirled with something vitriolic, something cosmic and caustic. Something unknown appeared to Mikalla and left just as quickly as it reared its glaring head. "Okay." The boy looked like he had been caught in a hurricane, eyes wide. He was helpless. *How should I react? How could I please Yolia? What should I say?*

And Gobi just stared at Mikalla with his jaw clenched, shaking. Yolia then turned toward the boy as well. It felt like a mountain sprang upon him, tumbling down and crushing him with attention. "You look confused, Mikalla. What are you wondering?"

"Um, nothing really."

And then it seemed like Yolia dimmed the lights with magic—of course, he didn't, but it looked as though the torches all around dimmed and dimmed just for him, channeling shadow energy to illuminate only his angry eyes. "Tell me."

"Well, *how* should I judge Gobi's story?"

"What do you mean? I told you," And instead of getting frustrated, Yolia just laughed at Mikalla's confusion. "Just," he said, nearly whispering, "do what anyone is supposed to do and say how you feel. Yes, say how you feel and how much you care." He smiled. "*That's* how you're going to judge Gobi's story. Got it?"

Mikalla nodded his head. Yolia motioned for Gobi to get up and stand in front of both The Conjurer and The Conjurer's newfound, lowly assistant. Gobi gave a sinister grin. Something goulish. Something wicked. Something snide and handsome and charismatic. Satanically white teeth. Hellishly glinting eyes. As he stood up, Mikalla could feel the weight of his steps and the grip of anticipation as he paused, paused for a while, before he showed a menacing grin, seeming to double, even triple in size by the glare of the barking flame. As his top lip curled into a smug arch, he stared at Mikalla a last time before beginning.

"A boy lived among many people—some who loved him, some who didn't. He had a family, and his family had some status. They weren't too wealthy, nor were they too poor. The boy passed people every day, worked with classmates every day, and spoke with teachers and parents and friends every day. He was never alone—always with someone. Yet in his heart, something told him differently. Yes," Gobi said, continuing and then suddenly turning his gaze back toward Mikalla who shuddered. "Somewhere deep down, he was alone as if there were a thin film over his eyes and mouth, preventing true connection. The only person he wanted the attention of, didn't notice him back—a girl he liked." Gobi seemed to—if only carefully and slowly—sway from side to side like a waltzing serpent. Mikalla had to stare at Gobi, predict where his hands were going to go, and then where he was going to step next. He was entranced.

Gobi only continued. "The boy was so lonely, in fact, and felt it so deeply in his heart, that alone every night he would sob and he wouldn't know why. Comforted by no one, he felt that he was different, like a worm among pebbles or a sprout among spiders—an alien." And then Gobi went deeper. He dug harder and with even more devastating precision into Mikalla's heart, into his situation, and into his psyche and soul like a dark mirror. "This boy—he knew no better. He only yearned. But what he yearned for, he did not know. The boy was like a ball of desire, unrestrained, untapped, and untethered, but with nowhere to go."

"That's enough with the exposition, Gobi. Now get on with the narrative. Remember what we practiced."

Gobi looked at Yolia with eyes of hot steel. And then he proceeded with his story. "Well, one day, the boy got noticed. Everything he wanted, everything he yearned for, it all seemed to come true that day. It was when an expert, a leader of the community, came to him and noticed all his talent and all his skill as a person. The boy felt like that hole in his heart was filled. He felt like it was all going to happen. His dreams were to come true, and his desires—however deep they may have been—were to be fulfilled."

Where is he going with this? Thought Mikalla. *What makes him this way? Why is this so much like what happened to me? Unless he's trying to psych me out. He wants to get in my head to play a game with me. A deadly game. Maybe not a game at all, but more of a hostile takeover of my mind. Where is this going next?* Mikalla swallowed and sat through the story, fidgeting, sweating, feeling a mudslide of fear wash over him. He was far from safe. He was watched, far closer than he thought he was. Far more intensely than would have made anyone safe, nonetheless comfortable. Something inside Mikalla shriveled up and died in that moment, replaced by a black dread. Some deep, primal fear welled up inside. *Has he been watching me this whole time? Have I been spied on? Is this a test?* His head spun. No answers. No light. No path forward. Feeling like his life was a dead end, a lie, he continued to listen to the story.

"The boy followed the man who noticed him, the one who saved him from his boring schooling and boring life. He followed him into his guild to see where he trained and where he worked on his craft. The boy was elated, no longer part of a stale life, but rather adventuring and learning and growing. It was his destiny all along. Or so he thought. Well, one day the boy, the leader, and the rest of the guild went out to a volcano to learn an ancient art. The leader insisted that they all get up close to observe the hot magma and to *feel* the heat on their arms and faces. And then," Gobi's face was lit by a flame, his smile was ghastly, ghostly, filled with some dreadful contradiction that made Mikalla shiver.

"When they all got close enough to the volcano—close enough to feel the heat and see the hot lava spurting and bubbling—the leader of the guild proclaimed they needed a sacrifice to the volcano to save the guild and the kingdom itself. It was the only way. And before he could notice, the boy was lifted up by everyone else, hoisted above the rim of the volcano, and thrown down to the heart of it. As he fell, he screamed, he yelled, and he cursed the leader and the guild and even his own life. But there was nothing he could do. He was simply done. Dead. It was destined to be nothing but a sacrifice. While the boy fell to his death in the mouth of the volcano, he could see the leader leaning forward over the rim, watching with no expression as the boy continued to fall, and fall, and fall. All the leader said was, 'you were only a means. You were just a pawn this whole time.' And with that, the lava engulfed the boy, his bones, and his longing heart. And with a chortle and a bubble, the boy was no longer. All that desire, only," Gobi said, staring and not blinking, stepping toward Mikalla, leaning down and looking into the boy's eyes, "to be used like a tool—his life amounting to no more than a simple commoner's."

Gobi put his hands on his hips. He puffed out his chest, which protruded even through his gaudy robe. "Is that the end?" Yolia said.

"The end."

Mikalla swallowed and couldn't help but shiver yet again. It was like his blood turned to ice and his throat turned to sand. His heart boomed and his lungs froze.

Yolia started clapping. And he clapped some more. He smiled and then kept his face stoic.

Gobi just stood there, knowing Mikalla was looking and feeling something he didn't understand. It was an attack. It was a bombardment. It was offensive in every way to Mikalla. But Mikalla didn't know what to do.

"Very well," said Yolia, "very well, indeed." The Conjurer then turned to Mikalla. Mikalla felt like a boulder fell upon his head with Yolia's eyes striking him. Strong and hard, Mikalla's heart became engulfed in flames, booming, beating, and pulsing. No amount of deep breaths could stop his shaking. His quivering. His scared shuddering. "So, Mikalla, what do you think?"

Mikalla only looked at the ground. "I'm deciding... I'm thinking."

"No," said Yolia, "listeners, commoners, readers—they don't decide. They don't think. They just feel. They just react. So? What's your reaction?"

"I—I don't know."

Yolia looked frustrated. "Well, let's start with the characters. The main one is the boy. Did you relate to him? I need you to react. I need you to feel, and I know you felt something."

Mikalla could feel, not see, Gobi's smugness, his evil knowledge of Mikalla's soul, and his leering and rearing. "I felt like I was the boy."

"Good! Good! Gobi, perfect!" Yolia hopped around like an excited child when he heard Mikalla say that. "What else? What else? Quick!"

Mikalla kept staring at the ground. "I felt like the boy was me. I feel like I'm in his shoes, like I'm misplaced. Like I'm alone or scared of being abandoned. Like I'm a sacrifice for something larger. I feel like I don't get the attention I deserve." Mikalla kept going on, spilling his precious consciousness for Yolia and Gobi. And the studio was deathly silent except for Mikalla's driveling voice. His eyes and soul went empty. "I almost felt," Mikalla said, then looking up directly at Gobi, "like it was *too much* like me."

"What do you mean? You feel like you're going to be thrown into a volcano?" Yolia wasn't getting it, and Gobi laughed.

"No, no, actually, I feel like…. I don't know."

"*Tell me*. Speak."

"I don't know," said Mikalla, "how about you say it, Gobi?"

"Who, *me*? I just told a story. I don't know what you're talking about. I'm glad you liked it, though." Innocence painted Gobi's face. He knew what Yolia didn't. He knew what only Mikalla suspected, and that was that he spied on him, watched him, complained about him, and plotted against him. *Gobi had to have thrown that rock. It's all Gobi. It's like he's everywhere. What am I supposed to do?*

"I don't know what you're saying, Mikalla. You don't look right. How about you take a break? Go wash up for a bit while I debrief with Gobi on his technique."

Mikalla put his head down and scrambled away as quickly as his heavy feet would carry him.

"But wait!"

Mikalla turned around.

"Gobi's baby, Mikalla—did you care for it?"

"A little too much."

***

Mikalla went back to his house later that night. He wouldn't tell anyone what happened. Not his parents. Not anyone.

"How was your day, honey?"

"It was good."

"Well, that's good. Did The Conjurer teach you anything special today? I'm telling all my friends at the workplace and they just think it's *amazing* that you're his assistant."

"Yeah," Mikalla sighed. "It's cool."

"By the way, we went to officials to let them know about the rock. They said they would try their best to determine who it was and keep extra watch for the next few nights. Don't be scared, honey."

"I'm not, mom." But he was scared. Not of stones but of eyes, prying eyes. Gobi. *That smile. That story... What does it mean? They'll never find out who it was. But I know. Maybe he's watching me right now....*

"Hey," his mother touched him lightly on the shoulder. "Is everything alright?"

"Yes. Everything's fine."

And he went to bed that night with doubts in his head, and his mother's concerned face peering in through his doorway as the candles in his room dimmed and his eyes shut for the final time that day.

Becoming The Conjurer

"*Goodnight*," his mother whispered as she shut the door to his room, leaving the boy alone with his own mind full of dread.

It was a turbulent night for Mikalla. One full of sweat and strife. One with pain creeping in, onward and toward every pore and from every corner. Figures cloaked in black, faceless creatures in the night with sinewy, red arms. Ghouls walking around and screeching. Dead, faceless things that were also alive in his head, more alive than anything else that night in his dreams.

Mikalla continued to float into his nightmarish dreamscape. His thoughts rippled and he had no control of his horrid nightmare. He saw all around him faceless things that resembled humans only in that they had two arms and two legs—nothing else. They hugged and groped each other. Shrieking. Black blood dripped along the walls. There was nothing to behold besides the shrieking creatures caught up in each other. His feet carried him into the middle of the black room. He tried to tiptoe, but he had no control. His heart was pressed and seemed close to exploding. A ball formed in his throat, preventing him from swallowing or breathing.

He cleared his throat, and then they all jumped. They walked toward him, all teeth and bodies focused on Mikalla, the only human left in the world, stuck in a void of a painting, the opposite of a place, a hole in space and time, a forever purgatory to which he was expelled just for being him. In the nightmare, he was subject to the chomping and chewing of the slurping creatures shrieking, devouring his flesh and feeling every bit of it. But before they could strike, one of the creatures in the back yelled something. The voice was booming and deep, but so human. It *was* a human.

"Stop! Everyone stop!" All of the faceless, gray creatures immediately came to a halt and looked back at the boy who yelled at them with such authority. He seemed to be their boss. Mikalla, then on his heels and with his back against a blood-spattered wall, turned to look for the voice as well. All motion halted in the room. The gray creature in the back reached his hand to where his face otherwise would have been and appeared to pull a gray film off. He removed a mask and then revealed the face of Gobi.

Gobi laughed in his usual voice, but his usual smugness was tinged with something more sinister. Something evil.

Gobi stepped through the crowd and stared at Mikalla. Mikalla gasped for breath. His hands against the wall slipped in black blood. He was covered in grime. He refused to look Gobi in the eyes.

"Mikalla," Gobi said, stepping closer still, "why do you think you're here? Why do you think you're trapped here with nowhere to go? Why do you think you're in danger?"

"I don't know. I didn't do anything wrong."

"But you did."

"And what was that?" Mikalla could still vaguely hear the gurgling whimpers of the faceless creatures. They listened too, and they hung intently on every one of Gobi's words. Every one of his twitches, every flap of his gums and lips. "What did I do wrong?"

"Mikalla, you crossed me." And then Gobi laughed like a child. "You crossed me, and you don't even know it."

"But Yolia doesn't want me to replace him. He wants *you*. I'm…" Mikalla looked down at his feet. The dream world rippled around him. "I'm nothing."

"You are nothing. I've trained for years. I've won awards. I've been groomed for this spot my whole life. I've learned, and in many ways, I've surpassed most." And Gobi smiled. His smile glowed and stretched far beyond his face. His words echoed through and from the faceless creatures like a cavern's call.

Gobi's face grew beyond even the room, and then in a chorus the creatures shrieked and yelled. "Do what is right, Mikalla. *Quit. Quit.* Quit and quit now. If you want a career in this kingdom, and if you want your life, quit being The Conjurer's assistant. Always remember that you're nothing. But I *could* make you something if you tell Yolia you quit. I'm the next in line to The Conjurer. I'm the king's nephew. Just quit now."

And all of his words and proclamations echoed again as Gobi grew into a giant. Grandiose visions. Mikalla tried to run but his feet were frozen. His spine tingled but failed to move a muscle.

"Sic' em," Gobi said.

And with that, the faceless creatures nodded at the call to action and crept toward Mikalla. All of them let out ghostly howls and their fangs dripped black blood. Mikalla yelled. No one heard him. No one cared. And in the void of a nightmare, infinitely alone and away from any help or care, he was devoured piece by piece by the faceless mob.

That was the last Mikalla remembered of his nightmare. He awoke the next day with violent relief and crushing fatigue, covered in sweat. Grateful, shocked, and scared. He had only one name and one face in his mind.

Gobi.

Chapter 12

The days following his brother's death crawled by. Beset with dark clouds, every word from his father felt like a hammer crashing down on his tired nerves. Full of apathy that burned and settled deep in his chest.

Oro's mind was in knots. *I'm going to be king. One day, I will sit on the throne.* He would spy his father talking to an attendant or commanding someone from his golden throne. *One day, that will be me.*

No matter how many times he repeated it to himself, he could not digest the fact that he was the first prince, the heir, and the next monarch to inherit the kingdom. But he did not dare vocalize this to anyone. Excitement was for happy times. This was not a happy time.

Everyone seemed to treat him differently now. His classmates stepped aside from him. He always caught them pointing and whispering. Wide-eyed peers were not talking to him or just pretending like he was some sort of statue or sacred deity. His royal adviser was the only person he felt he could confide in, the only person he felt would listen. Kitan was his safety raft. His confidant.

As an adviser, as a helper, and even as a friend, the longer Oro went on, the more he felt like Kitan was all he had. Kitan had a way of making Oro feel like he was the only one that existed. The universe's problems were similar to his. But Oro had to expand. He had to meet new people or do something to gain anything more than the little social capital he had.

Ever since his brother died, his father was removed. Removed from everything. His eyes lost their sheen. His hair, in only a matter of days, seemed to turn gray and brittle. His sleep was restless and his waking hours were filled with a kind of dull pain that ached with every step or sweep of his frail arms. Without Menizak IV, Menizak III was incomplete. Oro's father was a shell.

One night, they were having dinner. Around the vast table were only his mother, his father, and him. Little him. Oro's heart fluttered with an immature kind of rage, something in his soul that begged to be acknowledged. Silence loomed like a cloud. The air was thick. To all of them, the meal was tasteless. Bland. Utensils clanked every few seconds. The ceilings in the palace dining area were thirty feet high, making for a cavernous room that was empty with a fractured family inside.

Becoming The Conjurer

After some time, which felt like an hour, Oro spoke up. "How was your day, father?" His mother looked over at the man with the gray beard and hollow eyes. He barely chewed or breathed—a ghost of a king, a shell of a person. With food still in his mouth, he put his fork down. *Clank.* It sounded like a great drum in the silent cavern. Oro desperately wanted to get a smile from his father. A warm stroke of the voice, possibly. He wanted some sign or some indication that he was, in fact, the king's son. He wanted to believe that, even though his father was distant, he was just upset about the loss. He wanted something, anything, from his father. Some word or expression that would tell Oro that it would be alright.

He got none of it.

Instead, his father dropped his fork and turned his eyes to the sky. More seconds went by that felt like minutes. His father seemed not to have even heard his son's question. In some way, it was a cry for help. "Meni," his wife said, staring at the king, "are you okay?"

And then Menizak looked at his wife for a moment. His eyes were sharp. "Are *you* okay?" he asked with some sort of frustration.

"Your son asked you a question, Menizak."

"And I'm thinking!" His hand slammed the table.

The queen did not back down. "He asked you how your day was—what could there be to think about?"

"*I don't know*, Zaniyah. Why don't you answer it first considering you're so clear-headed tonight?"

Oro's mother took a small bite of the meal and chewed quickly. "He didn't ask me. He asked you," she said in a whisper. Oro's heart sank. Instead of the food that sat in front of him, he found himself chewing at the tips of his fingers until they went raw. He hyperventilated silently for fear of having his breath heard by his father. He tried his best not to give off a nervous sign. He didn't want to show any weakness as the first prince. But he didn't feel like it. He didn't feel like much of anything. His scared heart fluttered at his parents' frustration with each other. Pangs and spikes in his chest, tingling in his face, needles in his hands and heart.

"Well, Mother, we could start with you. How was your day today?" Oro grasped at something to quell the situation. He couldn't stand the pressure of conflict. Two humans fighting one another—*and over what?*

His mother's cheeks had hollowed out since his brother died. Her eyes went sad. Her brow sunk down to the top of the bridge of her nose. "It was okay, honey," she said softly. "I'm still taking it day by day."

His father sat there, his face sour, his jaw slack, and he appeared weak. He whispered something to the ground. It was inaudible. It came out as a wisp, unheard by the other two at the table.

"What was that, dear?"

"*Okay?*" The king said, shaking his head. His hands and teeth vibrated. "How could you be okay?"

"I'm—I'm not. There's nothing okay. How could you say that? How could you mean that and actually wonder?"

The king's voice raised a bit. It shook Oro's core. He shivered, as if a heavy, cold raindrop had plucked the back of his naked neck. His breathing got quicker. *I need to leave,* Oro thought. *Not another fight. I can't do this. I can't put up with it.*

"There's nothing okay. There never will be." Menizak III shook his head again. Quicker. And then again, with more fervor. His voice grew shaky, quaking with fear and trembling, deeper and then higher, and then deeper again. Quivering, he said something with a blank face that only death could describe. "We lost our boy."

Oro stared right at him and started to cry for a different reason. His father looked back at his last son with oblivion staining his deep, dead eyes. His mother pushed back her forehead and held her cheeks and cheekbones in her hands. She sniffed, and then Menizak said, "he's gone. All gone." The only way he moved was through his shaking hands and quivering lip. A dark cloud of dull and imminent pain fell upon the royal family then—scars too deep to mend. They figured it was never going to get better.

And it never did.

***

Oro left the table shortly after the tears fell. His vision was a myopic haze. He seemed to stumble about, searching for something that wasn't there and that he could never have. He had a hole in his chest, in his gut, in the thick of his soul. There was nothing for him to do. He didn't even have the energy to wallow.

He found himself downstairs after aimless wandering, way down in a deep cellar. It was dark and dingy, and it had a moldy smell that loomed thick and wet in Oro's nostrils. When he entered the cellar room, which was surrounded by large, musty stones, he heard the scuttling of rats. He lit a couple of the wall torches, illuminating whole shelves of bottles and barrels, all containing a rich, purple substance. It glowed in the light of the flame. It rippled at the might of his touch. His glossy eyes rested comfortably on its royal red color, that rich, pomegranate-dark sea of burgundy. *I see others drinking this and getting happy*, he thought. *Why can't I?* That was Oro's reasoning as he lifted his careful, cautious fingers to the edge of one of those bottles, uncorking the cap with curious pupils dilating. A world of wonders awaited. But with each sip, a world of pain and envy and the rich greed of the flesh also reared its ugly head.

He put the rim to his lips. Immediately, he felt some ungodly burn. The ripple across the cavern of his mouth stung with a vengeance. He reeled and nearly threw up at the first sip. But he held it in. And then he took another sip. Eventually, the burn lessened. Some wondrous flutter danced where the hole in his heart gaped a moment ago. The burn on his awaiting tongue began to feel like a healing sensation, more like a tickle than a sting. The sharp voice in the back of his head, yelling insults and doubts, faded away. The room spun like a merry ride on a stallion. The stones rippled, and the sweet burgundy wine settled warmly in his stomach. All his troubles melted away. His heavy, dragging face tightened into a crescent smile. He smiled and smiled. He couldn't *stop* smiling. This feeling was impeccable. It was perfect. His nerves softened as his face and back slacked, crumpling into a soft ball of happy, euphoric flesh. Everything around him felt good.

He got up from the stool and stumbled. His limbs were heavy and his mind was light. His spine waved in the imaginary wind of his drunkenness. He loved every second of it. And he continued to feel the drunken tingle of euphoria, clouding his vision until he drifted off into a pleasant, black dreamscape. Oblivion. What he wanted all along, he achieved.

Chapter 13

The next day at school for the first prince was a nightmare. His stomach churned in a fiery hell. His head pounded. His tongue felt like sandpaper. The backs of his sore eyes ached with a green feeling. It was the worst pain he had ever felt, and the worst part was that he could not tell a soul about it or why he felt that way. He couldn't tell anyone. He was alone on his own green island to feel out his hangover. Even water was an endeavor for his tired stomach.

He sat toward the back of the class that day, unusual for a first prince and even less common for Oro to do. But still he did it, and his head hurt the whole time and his joints ached with nasty venom. He raised his hand. "I need to go to the bathroom."

"You're excused, my prince."

Oro made it to the bathroom and didn't see anything or anyone. A violent spray. A sickening movement. *Oh my gods! This is horrendous. I'm never drinking that stuff again.*

After a while of sickness, convulsions, and violent green feelings, he felt a little better. At least he was good enough to walk and see straight. He got up from the stall and walked, but before he could get out of the bathroom, he saw a boy in gilded cloth, gold accents, and crazed patterns. A spray and a flash of color surrounded the boy. Oro thought he recognized him, but he hadn't seen the boy in a while. *Is he in my class? Why haven't I seen him in the back of the class lately? And why is he here now?*

"Hey," the boy said. He looked at Oro unlike he'd ever been looked at before.

"Do I know you?"

"No. I don't think so. Do I know you?"

And then Oro laughed a bit. It felt good for him to laugh. It was like a blast of fresh wind. "Of course you know me." Oro laughed again. "I'm the first prince." And then Oro's face went darker.

"Oh," the boy said and shrugged. "Anyway, I got you some water. I heard you in here…struggling."

"Thank you." Oro took the cup. "Why haven't you been here lately?"

"I'm, I guess, kind of, The Conjurer's assistant. I just come here sometimes on off days or when he feels like he should send me here."

"Oh, cool. My father works with him all the time. What's it like being around Yolia? What's Gobi like?"

And then the boy's face flushed. That was a name he did not want to hear that day. That was a name he needed a break from. *Gobi.* The boy looked at the ground. He seemed to shrink and shrivel away, shivering slightly.

"What's wrong?" Oro asked. "I'm the one that's supposed to be sick, remember?" he said, laughing and taking a sip of the water.

"Nothing. Nothing's wrong."

"I like your robe, by the way."

"Thanks. I wish I was able to wear purple like you."

"Well, why can't you?"

"I'm not a royal."

"Well, I am, and I say you can wear it."

The boy still had a blank expression. It was like he was staring into a void. It was like he had no awareness of anything in the present. Something traumatic, something lagging and congealing in his soul. "Thanks," the boy said.

Oro looked at him with an inquisitive stare. Both boys were frozen. Oro took a compulsive sip of water and then asked a question. "You're *really* The Conjurer's assistant?" he asked.

Something in Mikalla bubbled up. An oozing thought gurgled and begged to be let out. He hated that, and he hated the question that the prince just asked him.

"Well, are you?" Oro asked again.

Nick Oliveri

"Why would you ask me that?" Mikalla's clean hands clenched. His jaw tightened. A red blur marred the corners of his vision. It was inevitable. The anger seeped into his psyche too fast—far too quickly to stop. His breathing became audible. The boy had no idea what was coming over him, but he liked it. He savored it and used it and let the anger wash all over him. He hoped Oro had another snide remark to justify an explosion.

"I don't know," was all he could say. "I was just asking."

And then, through nothing and because of nothing—or maybe it was the weight of the incomprehensible world weighing on the string of his psyche—Mikalla snapped. "Well, ask again. Huh? Ask again."

"What?"

Mikalla's rage flowed through his raised voice. His face was a deeper crimson than even the drastic pattern on his ornate clothes. Red, red all around, was all Mikalla could see. "I said, ask again. Ask me again if I'm The Conjurer's assistant."

Oro's eyes were wide with fear. *Why is he angry? Was it something I said?* "I didn't mean to upset you." Oro looked at the boy, who had fire in his eyes and seemed to have it all over his body. But he remained so still. He just stood and looked at the floor. He had nothing but time. Standing there, he had nothing but time. Nothing around him. Nothing below him. No Oro, no floor or ceiling, and not even the feet he stared at seemed to exist. Oro noticed the boy was having a crisis. But he didn't know how to fix it. He witnessed his parents lose their firstborn son, and still, he had not seen someone so distraught, so sick with emotion, or lack thereof. The world had crushed Mikalla. Right from the outset and beyond, he was trapped. Oro looked at a boy defeated and confused, confounded by the enormity of the problems that sneak up on humans, animals, matter and then dust.

Oro felt Mikalla's distress at that moment. The boy did not need to say a word, and Oro knew he was suffering profoundly. "You know," Oro said, "I just lost a brother." He nodded his head slowly, staring into the same void as Mikalla was just then. "He was bad to me, but he was still my brother. And now I feel guilty and sick and scared of what's going to happen now." Oro continued to nod his head. "And I never asked for any of this. I never wanted it. I never wanted a brother, and I never wanted him to die. And in a way, I feel kind of trapped too."

Mikalla kept staring into the void. And then he looked confused. "Who said I was trapped?"

"No one. No one said that. I just feel like... maybe you needed to hear that."

Mikalla breathed for the first time in what felt like minutes. It was a stiff and deep inhale. He held it for a few seconds then sent it back out. "I'm not trapped. I'm never trapped." He kept staring into the floor, the void.

"I don't know. I feel like we're all trapped in some way. And I feel like you know that too."

Mikalla's voice escalated still. He shot up and held rage in his tight jaw. "What are you talking about? What are you trying to do? I don't care if you're the first prince; I don't care if you're anybody! Send me to prison. I don't care. Just stop talking to me." Mikalla got in Oro's face. He waved his arms. "What do you mean I'm trapped? What does anyone mean? Everyone just wants to put me in a box."

Oro backed away, but he knew he was in no danger. He knew, somewhere deep down, Mikalla would not hurt him. Mikalla would never hurt him. He couldn't. His heart was too pure. This outburst, to Oro, was something clean, something childlike and pure. For one reason or another, it endeared him even closer to Mikalla. He'd never had someone act this way toward him. He'd never had a peer disrespect him before. Everyone who he ever met cared about him. Cared about who he was. But this kid showed him no such respect. "Who are you, anyway?"

Mikalla looked at him. His face went from hot anger to opaque sadness, melting, drooping. "I don't know. I don't know who I am. How am I supposed to know that?"

The prince shrugged. "That's a good point." This seemed to disarm Mikalla. All Mikalla wanted to do was yell in a place where everyone could respect him and understand him. But he felt like Oro could. He felt like Oro got it. He felt like, for some reason, Oro understood. "But yeah," the prince sighed, "I miss my brother every day. I didn't want him to leave, but I never wanted him in the first place. Sometimes life just kind of does stuff around you. But you're not responsible for it. You don't have to be. I feel like, you know, you could just be who you want to be."

"But some people will. Other people, most people will."

Oro smiled. "You don't have to listen."

"Why are you telling me this?"

"I really don't know. I just feel like I have to. I feel like, maybe you needed to hear it."

Mikalla looked interested. His face changed. "What do you mean, 'I don't have to listen?'"

Oro shrugged. "I mean that you can listen to yourself. Believe yourself."

"Why don't you do that?"

"How do you know I don't?"

And they continued to go back and forth, back and forth in conversation. Both boys were stimulated and curious about each other. Oro desperately wondered why this boy was so indifferent to his royalty status. He figured, after some conversation after some time discerning and talking with this peculiar boy, that it was because he was deeply distressed. His name was Mikalla, and he did not quite fit in anywhere. His dream was to become a storyteller, and he had an urge to show people what he liked, what he valued, what he dreamed, and how he felt pain. Somewhere in the boy was a star. Oro couldn't quite understand it, but he grew to love it in that drawn-out conversation in that school bathroom. They talked and talked. And the more Mikalla laid out his visions and fears of the future—fears of Gobi, hatred for the box he was put in—the more Oro saw the star within him. He felt its heat and saw its brilliant light. It was so refreshing to meet an individual, someone who was scared just like him, angry and sad—confused just like him. They were both just boys that were taken for a ride on a thing called life and tucked into roles they never asked for, stuck in a box they desperately wanted out of.

"Hey," Mikalla said after some time, "we should do this again sometime."

"Do what?"

"Just…talk. About whatever. I enjoy it. It's fun doing this."

"Um, okay, I think I'd like that. We should probably head back to class now."

Becoming The Conjurer

"Oh yeah."

***

Mikalla and Oro came back to the classroom. On his way to the seat, Mikalla caught the most pleasurable flash of long, dark hair. Golden skin overlaid on a delicate collarbone, a long, thin nose; a long, thin body. It was Jani. It was the only thing Mikalla could focus on in the class. She was the center of his frollicking fovea. And she never paid attention to him. Not once did she speak to him. Never did she say hello or pass him a worthy glance. She looked forward, or at some of the wealthier boys—the prettier ones, the bigger ones. Only in his most vivid and terrifying fantasies did she ever think to speak to him or look his simple way. His clothes didn't help, his charm never got her attention, and neither being quiet nor loud ever made her glance. He did not know this girl except in his heart and in his mind's eye. This golden girl with marbled mocha inlays knew nothing of him. This euphoric princess. Never with a smile on her face. Always making him smile.

Maybe one day I'll have the courage to talk to her. To make her look my way. But what if she ignores me? What if I'm an embarrassment? And these thoughts of doubt and fearful, tearful yearning plagued his heart and tore at his lonesome mind. They corrupted his spirit, ate away at his very soul. It made him less of a person, a shell of a boy. Even the picture of her likeness in front of his seat from the back of the class brought him pain and joy supreme, longing for the distant, misted heights. He figured she was just that—a dream. Like his wish of being The Conjurer with Gobi and the society in his way, like the mess of nobles that sat in front of him, all richer and better connected, she was infinitely far away, a real person yet still only an apparition. *Jani,* he thought, hearing the voice in his head, *you're beautiful. And if I could only say so in front of your face. If I could only tell you just how beautiful you are—the shape being perfect—then I could be happy.*

But these thoughts that occurred just then rarely came up. They rarely surfaced in his troubled head for the pain they brought him. He could not let the hours tick away with her in his mind. He had to focus on desires that were less intense, on passions that burned lower and dimmer than the girl of his deepest dreams.

Jani tormented and teased him, pained and pleased him, all by doing nothing in particular except ignoring him.

The teacher was talking. Mikalla paid him no mind. He was normally an exceptional student, but it was so difficult to focus when his mind spun with mesmerizing secrets, while his heart ached with a chasm of longing, deprived of what he really wanted and lusted for: the girl with the long dark hair and dark eyes, mocha and cacao her complexion.

But something needled his consciousness. Something exploded his focus. His wafting dream crystallized, then shattered on the floor. "Mikalla." He heard his name being called.

And there it was again. This time, it was louder, with more fervor, as if to shake the entire room. "Mikalla…Mikalla!"

"Oh, I'm sorry. Yes?"

The whole class fell silent. Everyone's ears perked up, their attention and eyes fell upon Mikalla, all descending on the back of the class like a huge mudslide. Everyone looked. No one looked away or even seemed to do so much as to blink.

"Anyways," the teacher said, "I was explaining to the class why you haven't been around school as much. I wanted to talk about it a bit. Maybe explain the privilege conveyed to you."

That word stuck out to Mikalla. *Privilege. I'm…privileged.* A scourge of thoughts whipped through his head all in an instant as the teacher and rest of the class looked back at him. *How am I privileged when I'm surrounded by royals and kids richer than me?* Some burst, some pain, stuck him in the side. It rifled and stung and made an inaudible splash right on the side of his gut.

It was deep. It was sorrowful and insightful. He was hyped. He was elated.

"Um, yeah," Mikalla said, clearing his throat. His voice shrank, and then he caught Jani's eye. He saw something like fire burn in the irises of her marbled canvases. Her eyes, *her eyes. They're shining. At me. She's noticing me.* His voice got stronger. He cleared his throat and then released a haste of powerful words. "I'm The Conjurer's assistant." He heard ripples of approving gasps and saw jealous glares. "I work closely with him, as his assistant, judging stories and techniques and helping the replacement..." he cleared his throat again, "the next in line to gain his footing. I work with the myths and help form and judge them." He thought, and then he smiled, noticing the delicious attention of everyone in the room. He had them in his iron talons, unwilling to release the prey he had caught with a few simple words. But words, words gave him power. Words quelled his resistance and gave him hope. Words lit Jani's eyes with attentive passion, obscene and beautiful and lustful. "I gain insights from the gods now. I listen to the stories of the gods, their sacred myths, and I feel the pulse of the city, and I mold it and use it." He paused and looked around. Adoring eyes, evil lust, flashes of inspiration, and inquisitive stares all pointed toward him. "I am The Conjurer's assistant."

Becoming The Conjurer

The teacher smiled. He was proud. Having one of *his own* students be that close to The Conjurer made him happy. The class stared. Some of them began looking back toward the front of the room. All of them changed their posture. The teacher broke character for a second. "What is that like?" he asked. "What is it like to be with Yolia so often, working so closely with him?"

Mikalla smiled quickly and then stuffed the smile back down into his being, under his skin to where no one could see it. "It's like nothing else," he said. "I'm inspired every day, and I can't really say much more than that."

Mikalla glowed for the rest of the day. He loved the attention. He relished in the pleasure of praise. He loved the flowers that were thrown at his feet. He loved the compliments. "That's so cool," one boy said. "That's awesome." But most of all, for the rest of the day and into that night, Mikalla couldn't shake the vision of Jani's glowing eyes, stalking him, drinking in every word, her body facing him. He couldn't stop thinking about it. About her. *Her.*

She's beautiful. She's what the gods sing about. Her image melts my heart, crushes my mind, and brings me to tears and down to my knees. She's beautiful. And she looked at me.

Chapter 14

"I don't trust him," Gobi said. Yolia and he sat in The Conjurer's studio, alone except for one another. The studio was silent except for their words. It was dark, save for a few candles and the natural light that made the dust glow. Swirling. The gentle belch of the tiny flames lit all around.

"And why is that?" Yolia said. He had on a darker robe today than usual, all dark garments and dark bands around his wrist, with deep brown sandals. It was said that he dressed according to his emotions. He sought to express his inner life through his outer appearance. "It doesn't appear as if he's done anything wrong. He's a hard worker—a diligent and young one. I'm not sure if I see the same problem that you do." Yolia's mind spun with trickling fantasies of oddities, dark motivations, and the jealous intentions of those surrounding him. First, it was the king talking about Mikalla, making him question his very place and talent. And now it's Gobi. Judging Mikalla. Watching Mikalla. Accusing Mikalla. There was something about this boy they didn't like. And Yolia would get to the bottom of it. He felt he had to.

"That's not the point, Yolia. He has a demeanor to him, an energy that's...*off*. He comes from lower nobility, and his family doesn't have money. Who knows what he's liable to do? Who knows what he might, well, do?"

"I don't know either, Gobi. I really don't know what he's capable of." Yolia looked into the distance at the dusty flames obscured by shade. "But that's why he's here. He's here because I have no idea what he's capable of or what he can do. It's exciting. I seek to harness it. That mystery. He's a mystery."

Gobi looked flustered. His hands were on his seat. He squirmed. "We don't need mysteries, Yolia. We need predictability. I need to be trained. He's unnecessary. He's a disturbance."

"What's necessary, Gobi? Tell me. In this life and in this training—the training *you're* undergoing—what is necessary? You don't really know. And to an extent, I don't really know." Yolia inhaled and paused for a bit. "When I was in my training, I faced harsh trials—harsher than yours. I had people to beat, enemies to conquer, and challenges to overcome."

"I have too. I also had a lot to overcome. I've done that too."

Yolia gave a small laugh. "But of course, I wasn't the King's nephew."

Gobi got red in the face. Angered by a twitch deep within him. *I'm meant for this role. This is my job. I should already be The Conjurer. There's nothing I can't do. My skills have already exceeded Yolia's. They've exceeded anyone's, even the legends of old. I'm the greatest storyteller this kingdom has ever seen.*

Yolia spoke up again. "Do you have to say something?" He looked stern and his voice was flat and raspy. There was nothing pleasant about Yolia or his demeanor.

"As have I."

"What was that?"

Gobi raised his voice to a contentious level. Echoing, he boomed, "As have I. I've also faced challenges. I've also gone up against people. I've had to conquer and grow, and I *have*. I've done it all."

"Who have you gone up against in your training? Who have you outperformed? Who have you defeated thus far?"

Gobi searched for an answer. He tried to find someone in his memory who he had proven himself to. His mind scrambled. His legs quivered. His toes curled, and his jaw clenched.

Yolia leaned forward, not taking his eyes off Gobi. Watching him struggle. Watching him squirm. Watching him search for an answer he didn't have. Gobi knew it. Yolia knew it. He stared and watched Gobi melt under the pressure of Yolia's heavy questions. "Go against Mikalla."

"What?"

"I said, go against Mikalla."

"What do you mean by that?" Gobi was flushed with a dark feeling. Spiraling with abandonment and the void of oblivion, his deepest fears seeped into his reality. He was being challenged. He was being prodded. He couldn't stand it, and his whole body reacted with violence that he had to suppress. He had to stuff his feelings down and face Yolia's stare.

"I mean, I don't think you've faced enough trials to sharpen your skills and strengthen your resolve to the point where you should be."

Gobi was floored. "You don't think I've done enough?" He nearly yelled.

"I'm not saying that. I'm saying you haven't *faced* enough. Not enough people, not enough challenges. I want you to face Mikalla."

"In what?" Gobi's blood seethed with red, lava-like heat. "What say does he have? What has he done to even become your assistant? He's nothing!" Gobi stood up then. His chair fell to the floor, clanking and resonating throughout the room.

Yolia kept his calm the whole time. He continued to stare and watch Gobi's every move with a falcon's eye. "You're right in that he's inexperienced. You're right in that he's young. But he's not nothing—not to any extent. Mikalla is something, and that is very talented." Yolia said again, "*very* talented. And I want you to compete with him to see who can tell the best story."

Gobi swallowed and paced in a flurry of steps and flares. His mouth went in every direction. His eyes were crazed with panic. Fingers wild. He gulped air again. Then he faced Yolia. "You can't do this. You can't do this to me."

"Why not? What do you mean?"

"It's too late in the process for a competitor."

"Gobi, who am I?"

Gobi didn't answer. He just stared down at his own sandals in a fiery rage, controlled and content yet bursting at the seams.

"I'm The Conjurer."

Gobi shook his head. "You're a man in my way. That's what you are."

Grit teeth made of stained ivory procured Yolia's bared fangs. "You will not disrespect me like this. This behavior is unacceptable, Gobi."

"I will go talk to my uncle about this."

Yolia raised his voice, spanning his arms like the wings of a furious raven. "The king has no say in my process!"

"The King has a say in everything!"

"Gobi, come back here. Please, get back here. Don't walk away from me!" But he was gone, out of the studio and on his way to the royal palace to spill his anxious grievances all over the marble floor. "Insolent child. What have I gotten myself into?"

Yolia's mind became plagued with troubled thoughts. *My hands really are tied. I've been put into a box, and now I've lost all control. How did this happen? How did I get here? I can't even retrace my steps. How am I supposed to know what will happen next? It couldn't be my neck, could it? Could I really be punished for doing this?* Yolia's heart filled with the plaque of doubt and concern, black thoughts of death and a future dim and uncertain. There was hope, but maybe not for Yolia himself. He figured there was hope for something, though. Anything. Hope was all Yolia had as he sat in the chair and watched the door slam behind Gobi.

***

The king had glazed eyes from a night of relentless tears. He hid the pain from everyone, or at least he tried to. But there was no use in hiding his apathy or his anger at life and the forces that took it away so suddenly. He saw no point in it. There was no point to the loss of his son. He watched with sadness as a boy about his late son's age—it was his nephew—walk into the throne room with a kind of annoyed fervor. "What seems to be the problem, Gobi?"

"It's Mikalla. It's him again. He's getting in the way."

The king had a longing gaze, yearning for something he could never have again. "Getting in the way of what, exactly?"

"He's throwing a wrench in everything."

"Who is? Mikalla?"

"Yolia is. Yolia told me I need to be challenged more. He said I should 'go against' Mikalla. Meanwhile, he barely knows this kid. He's *not* qualified to be trained or to tell me how to train to become The Conjurer. He's just a kid from the lower nobility with no money. Yolia barely even knows anything about him. Now he wants to compare my stories to his? Compare me to him? *Him*? It's an outrage. A pure outrage. He doesn't even know what it means to be The Conjurer. He doesn't know how control works or how to properly guide the people. He knows nothing. And now, Yolia is telling me to—"

"Slow down, Gobi. Please slow down. Now, what is the problem? What is really going on? Tell me, and before you do," the king sighed. "Take a breath and relax."

Gobi stared at the ground. He wore a mad look of indignation, toxic, spun in venom. He reeled at the king's words. "How can I relax?" He whispered.

"What was that?"

"How can I relax," Gobi said, "when everything I love is being threatened? When the whole kingdom's mythos and all of the commoners' production and value hangs in the balance of a crazy person? And there's no doubt that Yolia's crazy. He's bringing Mikalla in to *compete with me*. After all the training I've been through, seriously?"

The king just stared on in apathy, a stone gaze set in stoic marble. He was only a figure, a shell, a statue then. He acted but he felt nothing—no nerves, no soft skin, no fond memories—only pain behind the eyes and ribs of Menizak III. Only a deep-seated, aching rejection of life coursing through his arteries and veins, all the way to his fingertips and back to his bleeding heart. "I know Yolia," The king said softly, still looking toward a fake distance. "I know him well. And I also know that he's only trying to get in your head. He's trying to test you. Trying to see what you're made of. Maybe he's right; maybe you haven't had a lot of tests."

"What do you mean?"

The king sighed again. He couldn't stop sighing. His lungs heaved with loss, his brow furrowed with anguish, every fold in his skin was a mountain of hatred. "I mean, maybe he's right. Maybe you actually haven't been tested much. After all, I don't see you day-to-day. I'm not The Conjurer. He is. His lineage has been appointed divinely, and therefore his process and his selection are divine." The deepest sorrow shrouded the king. He looked like he didn't care. Frankly, he may not have. He may not have cared about anything, plunging deeper into the prison of his own mind, petrified and annoyed at even his own nephew bringing a grievance to him. He was confused and angry and agitated, without the energy to express any of it. Only falling deeper into a depth with no bottom. "Maybe just stick it out. Keep at it. There's only so much I can do."

"And Mikalla? This boy, who has disrupted everything for nothing? What about him? He got pulled into all of this for nothing. He's not actually talented. He's not anything. He just acts and puts on shows. He's only a storyteller."

"That's what you're supposed to do." The king swiped his tongue across his teeth. "Maybe you could learn a thing or two."

Gobi looked off-put. A tornado of rage swept across his face, leaving traces of madness. Gobi was not satisfied with this answer. In his heart was fire. It filled his chest and gut and consumed him, all of him—his whole soul and everything that encompassed it. It ate at him. He looked his uncle in his lonely eyes and bit his tongue and the inside of his lip so hard he began to taste metallic crimson blood. Blood. It was blood he saw in his eyes, blurring his vision, blurring his emotions and decisions and his memories and desires. Within was a cage wrapped in a cage, boxed in, his bloody heart a labyrinth. There was no escape—that was the sentiment in his mind, chomping, skewering his torso like a bloody saber. Eating the decay, the healthy flesh, the coals of the flame that spewed in his gut. He saw blood. He knew blood was life, and he intended to take it and make it all his. Spill it into his cupped hands as a meal for life, hogging it greedily because he needed the blood. He lusted for it all from behind a blurred red tint. In the king's eyes he saw only his enemy. He searched deep in the abyss and found nothing. He hated it. He hated his uncle. He hated Yolia. He hated the vulgar commoners. Despised lonely people, scorned couples, and dismissed families. He hated—hated with a writhing passion, a violent quivering bloodlust—Mikalla. Life would be lost to him if he could not become The Conjurer. All life and everything he knew contained within the kaleidoscope of colors and impulse he knew as life would be gone, shriveled, turned to dust if he could not rise and control and express and be free. Finally, be free. Finally.

He couldn't wait.

The King spoke again. "And that is my word. Go now, my nephew. You are excused."

Gobi bowed and hid his glowering fangs while he did so. "Yes, Your Highness. Thank you, Your Highness."

Nick Oliveri

I thank you for nothing. I thank the world for nothing. I thank the parents who delivered me to this scathing wasteland for nothing. There is nothing. Nothing exists. Except for me. The stories in my heart. Those are real to me. My visions are real. My feelings are real, are vital and lively. I will impose them until the ends of the earth shrivel and the last maniacs die and the wretched sun sets for the last time. Then I will create a new sun. No, I will be the sun. And once I am the sun, there will never be night again.

***

Gobi sat in his room among his many drawings of the great Conjurer. Paintings of ceremonies, long scrolls and various poems and stories and myths, all of which came from his heart. He saw great visions of colossal stones, mammoth creatures in the black depths of ocean, murmuring and shrieking, tentacled things, only anger in the abyss. The deeper he sank, the more he was willing to do. *Mikalla will wish he never existed. He will regret the day he ever stepped foot on earth. He will want to turn back to dust the way I will make him writhe. I hate him. I hate him!* "I hate him!" he yelled. He saw only the worst in his head. The worst outcomes rear their heads in the worst shades of night purple and howling gray. He saw Mikalla's skinny face every time he blinked, every time he gazed too long into a painful distance. Everything would be dreary. He did not wish to live in a dreary world. He did not wish to do anything but be The Conjurer. For there was nothing, in his mind, stronger than the iron of his destiny. He would make it so. He would be the figure in the dreary night.

***

Mikalla liked to walk. His walks—morning or night, moist day or dry afternoon—were the place where he would sort his problems out. He could collect his runaway thoughts and keep his fickle heart from moving on too quickly or fleeing into a frenzy from the day's stresses. But when Mikalla walked he felt serene. He didn't usually go out at night, but he did at that time. Mist wafted, drenching the air in haze and frilling the moonlight in a silver gown. The elegant night paved brick in dampness. His steps plodded on. In the Inner Gardens, residents were always safe—always safe from commoners, at least. The mist puffed and flowed like a blanket in the air. Scratching, solemn night. Mikalla walked on, his mind adrift in a sea of ease. His feet seemed to drift along with his mind.

Then he heard something. It may have been a branch. It was more likely a footstep. It was a twitch of sorts, a disturbance that lit up the air. He felt it in his feet and vibrating within his delicate ears, trembling. And as soon and suddenly as the sound came, it left. It vanished in the nighttime fog.

Mikalla looked around. There was nothing. Nothing to see but the mist, nothing to hear but his own steps. He kept walking. His thoughts floated, slowly, back to playful fantasies and high visions of a good future. Dreamscapes drifting. He walked on. His steps clopped and made hard, damp sounds on the paved brick. Past buildings, past monuments and statues of old. Past windows dark and towers high. He walked.

And then he heard the same sound. It was closer, coming from behind him. Something desperate and creeping like a person was near. He shook slightly and for a while. He couldn't help but shake.

The sound came again. Mikalla jerked his head around, searching desperately for some sign of a stranger or someone, anyone, but he found nothing. Only the chill of night swept through his bones and trickled up and down his spine. Ice was in the air. His heart graduated to a nervous flutter. The dreams did not seep into his consciousness. His thoughts didn't float away. His thoughts were no longer adrift. Instead, he stayed alert, his nerves taut with static. His ankles were flexed and ready to flee.

But he found no one to flee from. He opened his ears and heard nothing again. Only the silent goran of dreadful night was audible.

He walked on—this time slower, with his back arched and his head on a swivel. His steps were hushed. His ears opened. Nothing. Nothing to hear, no one to see. His breath stopped for a minute, his eyes unblinking. *What's going on?*

He kept walking, going around a path and turning back toward his house. But he was still a mile away. The blanket of night felt heavy. His footsteps picked up to a slight jog. Hopping. Fear. A rhythmic beat to his heart that drummed and drummed to his fleeting steps, speeding up to a run, a sprint. No sound passed but the wind and his damp steps. But he sensed something coming or going, following him like a scent follows fresh bread. Someone watched with agitated glee his fleeing footsteps. Like water's cohesion with itself, someone stuck to his trail.

There was a half-mile to go. He slowed down as his thoughts speeded up. *Where is this person? There it is again! That sound, those footsteps—they know where I am. Gobi....*

And he heard the sound again. The multiple steps were like shots in the dark. He spun around, swiveling, shaking, running in place, and then in different directions. He couldn't find the culprit. He thought he heard a voice. No person was spotted. But no mistake was made—he definitely heard something. And the wind howled in an instant as he started to sprint. And his legs ate at the road with ferocious speed. He heard steps that weren't his, lurching, approaching.

There was nothing to do except run. Run and run some more. His lungs tanked and his eyes blurred with quicksand vision. The creases of his robe were like sandpaper to the brushing arms, swinging and flailing about. Steps were a dance with the devil.

He shivered in mortal fear. Ran again. He shifted his body like a spider does under deep and urgent duress. Mikalla never asked for this. He never asked to be pursued, but the path he desired and the path he took begged for it. It was inevitable, just as the night follows the day, smothering the sun in twisted obscurity.

He sprinted and could almost see his house. He ignored the blisters that were forming on his feet.

And then the footsteps came. Mikalla shrieked. He let out an otherworldly, glass-shattering screech. It was guttural. It was primal. And then, with his house in sight, Mikalla's sandal caught a paver in the road, and he fell head-first toward the ground with only his arm to break his fall. He ignored the running blood over his wrist and cheek. He sought only a closed door. But as he got up, a figure made purely of shadow streaked by. The robe of the stranger traveled so fast that it swept his hair to one side.

And that was the last thing he remembered before he was carried inside by a nearby guard that was patrolling nearby.

His head hurt the next morning. It was like a series of scrapes and pounding aches plaguing the inner lining of his skull, writhing and worming through the pink folds of his delicate and all-important mind. He had a bump where he'd been hit. Hit by what, he didn't know—foot or fist or sandal or rock maybe. But besides his pounding and pounded head, he was relatively unscathed. Only the rash left on his arm and cheek from falling down remained on him as remembrance of that one black night, that one figure cloaked in a dentless void with hateful vengeance on his or her mind. But Mikalla figured he knew who it was. He figured it was Gobi or one of Gobi's minions.

He figured a second thought, scarier and far darker than his initial conclusion of who hit him in the head. It was that he was always being watched.

He could have been under surveillance by one of Gobi's many royal tendrils, or possibly by Gobi himself. He was always being surveyed. *But why? Why this scrutiny? Why bodily harm? What did I do to deserve this?* He was only The Conjurer's assistant, but seen as a definite threat all the same. *But I'm not going to take his place. Yolia knows I'm not, and I know I'm not. If it really were Gobi, why would Gobi do this to someone who isn't threatening him? No. It has to be him. Those furious eyes and those hateful looks... the jealousy.* Mikalla shuddered at the thought. His life was in danger. His family was in danger. And clearly, nowhere was safe.

And how would he triumph over Gobi? Maybe he couldn't, or *maybe the best thing to do is let him win. I can't go through this again.*

As the morning sun took on greater strength, he heard his mother's voice. It was woven with deep concern, a confounding and anguished expression of distaste. She yelled. Mikalla shivered the whole time she spoke. Urgently, she talked to one of the guards.

"First it was the rock through the window, and now this? What's the meaning? I thought you said you were going to check this out. I thought you said you were going to investigate this. What happened? Where are we at now? My son could have *died*." In a violent yelling tone, Mikalla could hear his mother whimper. A torrent of emotion swept through him, burning the backs of his eyes already with the pain from the injury to his skull. "Oh *gods*." Mikalla could hear her crying. "I thought this was a safe neighborhood! I thought the Inner Gardens were protected and not just letting hoodlums run around and assault children. My child! *My* child!"

Becoming The Conjurer

And the yelling continued. It went on to a point where Mikalla felt bad for the guards. Mikalla felt himself squirming, scared, and tentative every time he moved his hand or twitched his foot. The pain in his skull throbbed. He'd never been apprehended before. Never even been hit or in a physical fight. This was unprecedented and unhinged. This changed his life and made him watch every step from that point on. This made his eyes always wander to the darkest corners of every room. This made him see the demon's face every time he blinked—that shadow rush of a figure in a plagued black cloak of night.

Gobi. Gobi everywhere. Gobi lateral to every step. Gobi looking down on every valley. Mikalla didn't know. But where he could have been was everywhere. Laced with uncertainty. Poured over with pain otherworldly, a prison of hell, in a life already of chains and aches.

Chapter 15

"Do you understand the opportunity, here?"

"What do you mean? Of course, I do."

"No. There's a whole world you're missing. You need to open your eyes to all the power you have as the first prince."

"And what is that? How would you know? It's not like you come from royalty."

"I don't."

"Then why do you know about my opportunities as a first prince? How do you know that?"

"Because," Kitan said, turning away from Oro while his face turned dark, "I know about power and leverage."

Oro nodded solemnly. He figured he needed to stick with Kitan. No one else seemed to have his interest like this peculiar boy from nowhere. No one seemed to confer the advice that could save him quite like Kitan.

And they continued to talk and talk some more. There was one theme that tied together all of their wandering tangents and conversational branches. It was power, and Kitan's musings on it as he spoke of its many tendrils and tools.

"I have a question." They were sitting on one of Oro's private balconies in the royal palace. It hung like a giant step outside of his massive quarters.

"Yeah?"

"What is power?"

Oro saw the searing words of Kitan in his head. They burned a space in his mind's eye. The question jostled and commanded attention. Oro, in that same instant, asked himself that. *What really is power*? He wasn't sure. He paused and continued to think. To really think. Think about leverage and force and what keeps people controlled. He didn't know. He couldn't discover the answer on his own. Puzzled, he told Kitan, "I don't know."

Kitan got up from his chair. His hands were behind his back. He wore the first silk robe he'd ever owned. It was black. He wore a stern face, his gaze was set in the future, drifting and aloof to a netherworld of thought and concepts. It was a world Kitan often traveled to and made his home. "Power is energy. It's math. It's figures that go back and forth." Kitan paced the granite floor, going back and forth in front of Oro.

"I'm... not sure what you mean."

"Think about it in a question. Who controls the energy of the kingdom?"

"My father."

Kitan turned around sharply. "*Maybe*. Maybe some. Maybe a lot of the energy he directs. But power, my friend, is fluid. It comes and goes with technology, with people, and with epochs of culture. It—"

"Where'd you learn this stuff?"

"You don't need to learn if you can think. And if you can think, then you can teach."

"Teach to others who can't think?" Oro asked.

Kitan smiled a snake smile. A varmint with a serpentine show of thin lips and long fangs. "Maybe," he said, "maybe. But regardless, that is power. And Oro, how is power controlled? How is it harnessed?"

"By force?"

"No!" Kitan said. "Force is only a tool. It is through suggestion that power is harnessed. True power is not derived from constriction but rather from *openness*. Suggestion, stories, hearts and *minds*, Oro. Hearts and minds. You need to get a grip on their hearts and minds. And who do you think has the power to control hearts and minds by *suggestion*?"

"The Conjurer." It was automatic, as if Kitan knew Oro would answer that way.

"Yes, Oro—The Conjurer. The Conjurer controls the hearts and minds of the people. That's what makes the whole world tick—hearts and minds. It's hearts and minds that build houses and towers and weapons. That's

Becoming The Conjurer

what hearts and minds do. They're everything. *Everything*, Oro. They dictate where you go, and they're going to dictate how you rule. So there by controlling The Conjurer, you can influence the hearts and minds before they influence you."

"But why would I want to do that? Don't I already have enough by being a monarch?"

"My prince," Kitan said, nearly laughing, partially growling, "you have to care about power; you have to attain power, because if you don't, you'll be crushed by the teeth of its ever-turning gears. And no one wants to get crushed now, do they?"

Oro understood fluently. He absorbed the picture that Kitan was painting. "Okay, you're right. So what do we do now?"

"It seems that you already know. You need to install another Conjurer. A Conjurer of your own."

"With your help?"

"With my help. With all the help you can get. We'll do it. We'll get someone loyal to you. Someone that you like."

Someone that I like. An image of a boy appeared in Oro's mind. He was young and fiery, misguided and troubled. He seemed to be gentle, loyal, and explosive. It was the boy he'd met in the bathroom. The one that didn't care whether or not he was a prince or a king or a monkey or anything else. *Someone that I like....* Oro liked that boy, Mikalla. He knew he already had talent, he already had connections, and he was already The Conjurer's assistant.

"I know who it will be," Oro said. "I have an idea."

"How?" Kitan said. He looked flustered. Oro had stunned him. "How do you already know who you want to try to install? Shouldn't we brainstorm first?"

"I already did," Oro said. "I already thought about it, and the picture's already in my head. It's Mikalla I want."

"Who?"

"Mikalla. The assistant to The Conjurer."

"Not The Conjurer's apprentice? The Conjurer has both an assistant and an apprentice?"

"Yes. And he's brilliant. The assistant is everything I want as The Conjurer."

"Okay, yes, but will he listen to you?"

Oro paused and looked at his feet. He couldn't ascertain the question yet again. He couldn't grasp what Kitan was getting at. But Oro, after a long time of staring and doing his best not to flinch or shudder, just gave the adviser a simple reply. "Yes. Yeah, he'll listen."

"Well, he has to if you're going to maintain power. It's your era—the beginning of it. You have to start now. As your royal counsel, I will begin working on that with your permission."

"Well, yes. But how do we go about this? What are the steps? I don't know the first thing about installing someone as my own."

Kitan paused for a while and waited. Oro waited with him. "You need to understand something, and I'm going to make this as clear as I can. You are now the first prince." Kitan pointed a finger at the boy who sat while he stood. "*You*. You have a responsibility. You also are endowed with a hammer of power, of sway and influence. It's yours to use. All you have to do is *swing it*." Kitan gritted his teeth as if he'd been waiting for this moment his whole life, save for the fact that he was only a poor boy a couple weeks prior. "I will teach you how. I will teach you to use that hammer, to swing it violently; to know when to wield it and when to keep it sheathed but shining still for everyone to see. I will teach you how."

Oro just nodded in appeasement. He seemed to hold something within like satisfaction, something happy, something gorgeous and fulfilled. "Okay," he said, fully trusting in Kitan.

And thus the partnership was born, cemented in a wall of trickling stones, damming the ever-flowing river of power and power's great diversions. They shook hands and looked out at the whole of the kingdom. Enlarged by the distant and endless sky, the city stretched for miles upon miles of marvelous creation.

Buildings and pathways and statues and markets, all providing the vital blood flow for the brain. Every person was a vessel. Every house was a cell. Every market was a vital organ in the body of the kingdom.

"In due time," Kitan said, leaning forward and somehow looking into the city's distant gaze with both disdain and lust, "this will all fall within your domain." He turned around. "And you need to be ready for when it does."

***

Mikalla walked outside the studio. Yolia and Gobi were working on costume design and instrumentals for ceremonies. They had Mikalla watching and listening and judging. And in a break from the action, Yolia told Mikalla to fetch them a pail of rich juice for a refreshment. "And make it extra concentrated," Yolia said. "*Oh,* and a lot of it, too. Get a bucket of juice for all of us."

It was broad daylight and Mikalla still felt out of place, on edge, within a realm of uncertainty and shadows and plagued air from a dark sun. He walked on toward one of the juice dispensaries that was only found in the Inner Gardens—nowhere else would there be such rich, concentrated nectar dispensed so freely.

Mikalla's head was on a swivel. He thought he heard a voice. *Not again,* he thought, before walking on and then pacing backwards, laterally, and forwards again. *Not again.* It was faint, a whisper in the wind. He could have been mistaken. It could have been in his head.

He turned around and he heard the voice again, faint and following a whisper. "*Mikalla*...."

Under his breath, Mikalla said, "who's there?" But there was no one to answer. There was no one to look after him, protect his head, or watch his back. It was only him. And then he picked up his pace again. And everywhere the wind mocked him. And with every step, his feet begged, yelled, and screamed to turn back to safety. Turn back to a place with no whispering wind. No calls from the shadows mocking him. The wheels in his head ceased to turn. They rusted from the panic. The sun turned black, and the pavement turned to sand. No motion felt good, and it all hurt Mikalla to walk and expose himself to another attack and the elements of uncertainty.

"*Mikalla*, you're not welcome. You should go back home before you get hurt." The wind whipped and the words of the phantom obscured. Mikalla shuddered and shed a tear. But that tear didn't matter. Nothing he did mattered much, he figured. And with every step, another tear—the only thing he could produce.

And then he cleaned the tears and anger from his face to order from the juice stand. Being smiled at, even by the man at the stand, gave him a morsel of comfort, a shred of ribbon to hang onto. But things weren't as they seemed anyway. Why should Mikalla believe one thing when they shifted constantly, constantly a tremorous storm, immediately a hesitation, a burden that had to be waited for.

He walked on with the pail of juice in his hand.

"Come again!" The juice man said. Mikalla flinched. He had a smile on his face. Mikalla wore anxiety on his eyebrows, weighing him down much like his right hand that held the pail. He shuddered after he flinched and swept his head around to look at the man who just waved at him.

Mikalla's heart raced, but he had not the wherewithal to realize that or anything within his body; all of his awareness was pointed to the black skies and the glooming drip of the fresco of his vision,vision, where melting paint blurred what he could see. He breathed heavily and slowly.

Yolia expected what he expected in himself—greatness, purity of heart and mind, and a devastatingly sharp and focused work ethic. Mikalla was generally a sharp and focused person. A kid with passion unbound, a future bright with the flames of unbridled passion, a fleeting chain of destruction and creation. But lately,

Gobi and the swirl of threats in his bruised head have tormented the innermost compartments of his mind.

He walked on and was forced to a slow pace with the juice in his hand, sloshing and full of nectar. He could see flashes in the corner of his eye under the blanket of sky. Vision dark and blurred by the figures he once saw that night and now continues to see. And then a face every time he blinks: Gobi. The smile, the envious grimace pointed all at Mikalla, shuddering.

The studio seemed so far away. His feet felt so heavy. His breathing was hard. It became a chore to do anything and soon he naturally took a break to catch his racing thoughts, his runaway mind, being chased away by a predator unlike he had ever gone up against. *What's the meaning of this? I'm trapped. I'm trapped and I never asked for any of this. Gobi chases me and tortures me with glares and ridicule at every turn, yet I've never threatened him. I never asked to be gifted. There really is no escape.*

Mikalla would have cried, but he did not have the strength to shed a tear—his eyes were too tired from seeing an unfair world at the precipice of adolescence and from being a piece of a puzzle set he hadn't yet found. He was confused about why he was that way, spiraling and feeling dizzier without the pail in his hand.

Nick Oliveri

He sat down next to the pail and focused on his breath—it's what his mother always said to do when he was feeling stressed and wanted to sleep or relax.

The studio was in sight then, but he had no means of getting there. He had no intention of walking through those doors with the juice in hand and his mind in that condition. *What's wrong with me? Maybe Gobi's right. Maybe I don't belong here or anywhere. Why did Yolia want me in the first place? Why would anyone want me?*

The darkness plagued him and sat on his shoulders. So young. So much talent. He had so few options in his head, and he *needed* options. The fresco painting of all his surroundings continued to darken and drip.

But there was a glimmer. There was a ray of light not black, brown, or purple but bright white, the color of peace. The color of hope. There was a wave of feeling as he saw himself, above and surrounded by a crowd. He felt the emotions of his pain captured by people everywhere. Reception, belonging, and something warm like a hearth comforted the torrent within his soul. He felt the wind of certainty for only a moment, but a moment was all he needed. He was certain or unshaken about something he couldn't quite grasp, but he saw and felt it all the same. The world soon stopped melting, and the dark fresco of his surroundings no longer dripped with violent lust, but crystallized into the bright world he used to know as a young child.

He took one last deep breath and smiled. He picked up the pail and headed back to the studio. As he approached, he felt the immensity of the situation and the battle at hand. Around the building was a presence drawing him in—attention from a higher power beckoning him toward destiny.

When he walked in, both Gobi and The Conjurer were focused on something else—playing an instrument or talking in between noises that emanated. *Everyone is so bent on control, whether it's controlling others, controlling instruments, or controlling the story at hand. I could never look at a person as an instrument, to be played or controlled.*

"Hello guys," Mikalla shuddered at the sight of Gobi, but had on him a smile and around him a newfound sense of calm after his epiphany on the ground. He was ready. He was prepared for attacks, hardened with a peace whose origin was not apparent. Sent from the gods a gift of light, a fire, a flare, flickering within him. "I got the juice."

Yolia turned around from his work and told him to put it on the bench over there. Gobi sneered to himself. Mikalla felt the dark presence.

"Don't drop it," Gobi said as he stared at Mikalla with callous eyes.

"We're working on the ear today," Yolia said. "Fine-tuning the experience to seduce the person, to grab attention and command respect—to keep a butt in a seat and plant their feet. This is important, Mikalla, but I just want you to sit back and watch as I show Gobi. Both of you can ask questions at will. Stop me if you're confused." And Yolia went on, demonstrating, handing the instrument back to Gobi, and then demonstrating again. The morning ticked on to midday with this cadence in a similar step throughout. But the storm was no longer in Mikalla's head as he watched Gobi begin to grasp the instrument and its delicate heavenly sound.

Mikalla thought to himself, *I will be just fine.*

Chapter 16

The palace's grand ceiling in the throne room towered over both the king and his son, the first prince. Oro's eyes burned whenever they passed over the shell of a man who sat on the throne, weak and skinny and bearded. He called this man his father. And everyone called his father the king. Menizak III sat while Oro stood. They faced each other. While Oro's head was full of doubts, plans, and worries, his father's mind seemed to be blank, set on nothing, and bent on nothing in particular. Oro approached, doing his best to square up.

The king scratched his head. They exchanged pleasantries, and then Oro got down to the point he wanted to make. He felt almost like a predator stalking apathetic prey, an awaiting target. But he had no idea how this would play out. Oro gulped. "Since I'm going to be the king one day, I'm just trying to get a grasp on a few things."

His father gave the slowest nod he'd ever seen. "Very well."

"It's about appointments. How did you choose your court?"

And his father answered. It was a long, weary response, drawn out by fatigue of the heart. It was basic and bland, and Oro came to expect a lot of what his father said, going down the list of all of his courtiers and cabinet members and explaining how they got there. Oro listened closely, no matter how boring it got to do so.

And then Oro fired another question. "What about The Conjurer?"

"What?"

"The Conjurer. You didn't mention how you appointed him."

"That's because I didn't."

"Then who did?"

The King on his cold throne gave the closest thing to a laugh that Oro had heard from him in months. "Son, the king doesn't choose The Conjurer. The people don't even choose The Conjurer."

"Then who does?"

"The Conjurer himself chooses his successor."

"Why was Gobi chosen?"

"Because he's talented. Because he's divinely appointed."

"But surely you had a say in it?" Oro said in an inquisitive tone. "After all, he is your nephew. Don't you have absolute control over the narrative, anyway? This all seems so confusing."

"Slow down, my son. One at a time. Control yourself. Now, what is it you're asking? Are you asking about Gobi?"

"Yes. I am." Oro took a breath and looked down. "I want to know how he got there. I'm curious and feel like I have to know if I'm going to be in your seat someday."

The king nodded but continued to stare into the distance. His infinite gaze was punctuated by long pauses of his eyes retreating into their lids like the sun sets down, slowly, invisibly, underneath the hills and oceans. He was still stolid. "That makes sense, of course. But Gobi was only in position because he happened to be a noble—a commoner can't and has never been The Conjurer for as long as this kingdom has existed."

"Okay, so why Gobi over all of the other nobles?"

"Yolia chose him. There's nothing else to say." The king leaned his large head on his tired hand.

"And how did Yolia choose him?"

"No one knows. You'd have to ask him, but he'd never tell you the entire process. There's no way of knowing for sure. The powers that be, they're secret, hidden even from me."

"So you don't have a handle on that?"

"No king ever has had a handle on The Conjurer. Our forefathers have tried, Oro, but there's no telling.

There's no way to see behind the curtain. I've tried. But I can only talk to him. I can only suggest. Commands don't really work with The Conjurer. The entertainment of the people, the stories of the kingdom—they come from a different power, something bigger than all of us. No one understands it except for The Conjurer."

"So what would happen if you tried to command The Conjurer to do something specific that he didn't want to do?"

The King cleared his throat and adjusted his space on his chair. He couldn't seem to find a comfortable position, constantly fidgeting and searching for something right. He'd thought about this before. The relationship with The Conjurer. How much power Gobi had as the chosen successor, divinely and secretly appointed, versus the current Conjurer, versus the king, and the people themselves. The swarms of them that had the stories in their minds. It was the many people that had the power to change things. It was the people with all of the say. But maybe the power came from making them realize they had nothing to change. That the forces at play are larger than them and loom over the kingdom like a cloud from the heavens, a force of the very wind and nature they could never hope to control nor change, but rather just to be a part of.

"Here's how I understand it, Oro: everything influences The Conjurer, and The Conjurer influences everybody. He is the divine storyteller. He is the most skilled interpreter of our world and its aesthetics, its mechanisms, its, well, whatever. Is The Conjurer divine? I don't know. Is his power divine? In a way, yes. Yes it is. The Conjurer has the divinity of the gods as a messenger that also goes above everything. After all," the king said, "it's not me the people love, but rather the stories about me. It's the stories that move mountains."

Oro took a while to take it all in. He just paused and stared too, trying to comprehend what he had just been told. It was as if a veil was lifted from above his eyes, seeing the world past the tinted, obscured film of his childhood. "Okay," Oro said after a while, "and who was the original Conjurer?"

"There's a story to that," the king said, "but are you really going to believe a story? The same story that controls people and propagates other stories, all connected to something we can't understand?" The king bit his lip.

"I guess not," said Oro, like a sponge soaking in every last ounce of wisdom his father dropped during his rant. A picture of Mikalla flashed in his head, and he realized that The Conjurer, Yolia, was still just a human. He realized that Mikalla was all too human, and that Gobi had desires just like them, just like anybody. It would take effort to bring Gobi down, but that effort would be worth it, according to Kitan and also according to Oro's inner belief. Gobi had to go. And there was no one way to get rid of him, just as there was, seemingly, no one way to become The Conjurer.

The two spoke for a while longer. The father and son. And for a flash—at least, Oro thought—he saw his father smile. Happy and proud to still have someone to whom to pass on his knowledge. Oro couldn't be sure, but he suspected that his father actually *enjoyed* their talk.

A warm feeling simmered in Oro's gut as he walked out of the throne room to go and report his findings to Kitan. His vision, his idea, would have to play out at some point. And Oro felt an excited danger he had never considered before.

Maybe he would have to pay for his actions. Maybe even a body would drop. But something had to change. He was the first prince now, and that flash of a smile from his father told him it was time to take the reins of his own future.

Treacherous thoughts and betrayal plots wafted through the air of the pristine Inner Gardens.

***

Yolia, Gobi, and Mikalla sat in the studio. It was the end of the day, and the end to a session that proved to be much needed for Mikalla. Mikalla yearned for an end to the glares and passive threats that floated from Gobi's deceitful mouth.

"This weekend," Yolia said, "we have a ceremony."

The word echoed in the walls of Mikalla's panicking, choked mind. *Ceremony. Ceremony....* Of course, ceremonies were what defined The Conjurer and his role. It was during ceremonies that the hearts and minds of the kingdom were molded, lit, and sculpted for rejuvenation. Everything happened at the ceremony, where The Conjurer would conduct the stories projected as shadows onto the side of a mountain for the whole kingdom to see.

Yolia continued. He spoke of wind and song, of the myths they've practiced and the ones yet to be explored. "We're just going to do as we've practiced," he told Gobi, looking directly at him. "And this time, you're going to help me out on stage." At that news, Gobi's face glowed and showed through with gold and a bright smile. Levity opened his heart at that moment. His face sang with the beauty of rare contentment in a world rife with deprivation. Mikalla had never seen Gobi so happy.

Everything about that sequence of events made Mikalla sick. The news gave him a sinking feeling. It was a guttural phenomenon he was familiar with. His own inner compass felt brittle and stagnant, paper-thin and deceitful. Mikalla's whole world swirled as Yolia and

Nick Oliveri

Gobi stared at one another, smiling, talking about the ceremony and planning its every intonation, right there in front of the sad assistant. Mikalla stared at the outer crust of his dream through myopic vision. It mocked him. The Conjurer had no idea the pain he caused Mikalla. But Gobi reveled in it, and he knew very well how this celebration and jubilance between master and apprentice made Mikalla, the outsider, feel.

"Great," Yolia said. "Mikalla, you're dismissed. Great job today." And with that, Mikalla walked outside. He plodded on, out of the studio, still hearing the snickering and guffawing of the collaborating duo, Yolia and Gobi. *Why do such bad people get to such high places*? Mikalla asked himself. He felt like he should have gone home right then, like he had a pull to some place quiet to cool his nerves. But he had enough alone time as it was. He was lost in plain sight, lost in familiar territory. Mikalla spun, taking steps in all directions, not knowing where to go. He asked himself another question before he answered it. *What does my life mean? Basically nothing. I'm one of millions, another tool to help the gears turn forever and ever. Flung around. Cast aside. And I can't even enjoy my own pitiful life.* Mikalla looked around flippantly, still very much in his own head. *Do you see any of your friends here, Mikalla?* A tear stroked his eye on a razor's path. *That's because you have none! That's because you only have yourself, and that's never been good enough. Look at all the other kids, out there playing and laughing and partying…. You don't do any of that. You think you're destined for greatness, you think you're talented, and then you get stuck at a dead end with your impossible dream hanging in front of you like hopeless bait. It's absurd. It's unattainable.*

He kicked an innocent rock that laid on the ground next to where he stood. He wished that rock could have said something. He wished it could have reacted with reproach or even a simple "ouch." It didn't. Instead, the rock just rolled and scattered dust, hiking through the simple ground until it slowed down and nicked the ankle of a person that walked toward Mikalla.

"A little old to be playing with rocks, no?"

Mikalla didn't say a word. He was frozen in fear at who he just kicked a rock at. He swore he didn't see him. And then, like a snake out of a dirt pocket, this man appeared. *Or, is he a man? He looks more like a boy, an older one—older than me.* And he was, at least, older than Mikalla. His robes were black but embroidered discreetly with some pattern Mikalla couldn't put his finger on. The teenager was skinny. Very skinny and relatively tall, slender in every regard. His eyes were sharp like fangs, and his slight smile spelled out a million words, impossible to be deciphered clearly by anyone. He was in the daylight, but this man was completely opaque. With hair long—as was against the customs of nobility—he was shrouded in careful, cautious, calculated defiance. Self-worship abounded out of his mouth, tumbling onto the ground by the rock and through the wind to reach Mikalla's scared ears.

Mikalla jumped at once. Slightly, as if not to be noticed. But the man noticed everything. He watched Mikalla. "What's your name?" the figure asked. He poured over Mikalla's likeness, noticing every inch and picking up on his every twitch and shudder, only causing more light tremors in the boy's fluttering heart.

What's going on now? Another thing outside of my control, flinging me elsewhere? What's happening? When did my life get so complicated? I don't deserve this. Mikalla shifted and shuddered to himself. "I'm sorry, but who are you? May I ask?"

"My identity is not necessary until I learn your name. I'm looking for someone specific, and if you're not him, I better be on my way. Did you not walk out of that studio just now?"

"I did."

"Good. And what's your name?"

"You're looking for someone who works in the studio?"

"It would appear that way, wouldn't it?" The figure in black became agitated, his voice laced with something of speed and quiet discomfort. "Now, allow me to get your name so I can be on my way and stay out of yours."

Mikalla liked that proposition. He appreciated the teenager's politeness. He caved. "My name's Mikalla."

The man's eyes lit up. His mouth grew wide with grim joy. "Very well. Very well, indeed. It would appear this trip was not in vain after all. Come with me."

"Woah, woah, wait for a second. Who are you? Why are you here? Where are you taking me?"

The figure in black smiled some more and just stared at Mikalla for a while. Looking up and down, up and down, and giving Mikalla the jitters in the process. "Curiosity," the teenager started, "is a powerful drug. You best not overuse it."

Mikalla sneered. Suddenly, this interaction went south. *Who is this kid to tell me what I do and what to do? This is madness.* "Okay," Mikalla said through a strained breath, "I'll be on my way now." And he picked up his shoulders and began to turn around.

"By a royal decree of our great kingdom's first prince, you will not be on your way. In fact, and by royal decree, you will be coming with me. Now."

Mikalla's mind went everywhere, but his mouth didn't move. He stayed in place, considering everything and acting on nothing. His jaw seemed to hang limp. Shocked and frozen, he maintained only a whisper.

"Okay." And he followed the man, who was not much older than him but still grown and eerily adult for what his age seemed to be. He was an enigma of the highest quality, something too thin and difficult to grasp. After a few steps, Mikalla passed off a humble question to his escort. "So, what's your name?"

"Kitan."

***

Mikalla had never been to the royal palace before. But in its usual fashion, his life took an unexpected turn off the rails, in which he found himself just there, *exactly* there, at the side entrance of the king's royal palace. His jaw could not drop any wider. Mikalla was led through hallways and onto spacious balconies. The walk became more of a marathon. Kitan asked him questions the whole way there.

"So, who are your parents? What do they do?"

"They're clerks for the government—both of them."

"Any siblings?"

"No."

And the questions continued to descend deeper into Mikalla's heart and life, into the parts of his spirit he would have liked left unexplored.

"What has it been like being The Conjurer's assistant? You're up close with him often, no?"

Mikalla knew nothing about the guy. He figured he was just there to escort, with nothing to say. But Mikalla had no idea. Mikalla never asked *him* any questions of his own. He was far too scared to and far too confused to mess up a time where he actually felt listened to for once. He would find out soon after they stepped into the prince's private quarters.

A miniature foyer greeted them while a servant displayed a platter of cacao drinks for them to indulge in. Mikalla's eyes widened at the delicacies, the layers of privilege frilled on one another richly, everywhere a gilded corner, everywhere a handmade detail, nowhere a discomfort in sight. And then a familiar face appeared from around the corner of a wall. It was—as Mikalla expected—Oro, the kid, the prince he'd met in the bathroom that one fateful time. Mikalla looked at himself and at everything in that moment through a dreamlike lens. Some whimsy on a ride he couldn't control or tame.

Oro had only warmth in his smile. "Mikalla," he said, arms stretching out wide, "come this way, this way. It's great to see you again." Hugging Oro was like hugging a bear cub. "Come, we have much to talk about."

Mikalla had his eyes on all of the luster and decadence of the grand room, but his mind on Kitan. *Why is he still here?* Thought Mikalla. *He's staring at me...studying me, a little like Gobi does. Why? What's going on?*

Mentally, Mikalla had a thick wall up, surrounding his heart, his wants and wishes. *Is it even worth it anymore? To have my guard up? To stand and fight? To protect myself from what's inevitable because of forces and people outside my control?*

"Yeah, come sit," Oro said. He pointed to three grand chairs in the vestibule of his giant, high-ceilinged bedroom. The chairs were oak or mahogany, or some rich type of wood that stood sturdy and resolute under warm bodies. "Mikalla, it's great to see you today, it really is." They all took their seats, Mikalla and Kitan with their cacao drinks, and Oro with a chalice of his own containing an unidentified liquid. "I'm assuming you've met Kitan," Oro said. "You two will get along just fine." Oro adjusted his pudgy rump in his seat. He squirmed as much as one could in a stationary chair and went on, being the only one talking or moving in the dense air of the room. Never was there a lonelier three than them. They sat together, but in solitude. The three of them—Oro, Kitan, and Mikalla—knew what it was like to be alone, abandoned, traded in to the whims of the world with nothing more than a rickety raft to cling to amidst the waves of being and non-being. The three of them combined their loneliness, each with a solitary agenda stronger than the sum of their unequal parts. What terrifying creations would they bring to the world? "I must ask," Oro continued, smiling and fidgeting, "what are your impressions so far?" He stared at Kitan.

"What do you mean by that, Your Majesty?"

"Well, what do you think of the kid, my friend?"

"You mean Mikalla?"

"Yes! What are your thoughts?"

And an awkward air pervaded the room and tested those present. It simmered right under Mikalla's nose, shocking and chilling his torso. *What's he going to say? What is there to say?*

Kitan gave a small, glib smile for a moment. He shifted toward Mikalla, revealing eagle eyes and hungry fangs. "He's good," Kitan said, lifting his thin, sharp eyebrows, "he's smart." Nodding, "strong-willed. It's going to take a bit to tame him." And then Kitan laughed and patted Mikalla rather hard on the side of his arm. "I'm just kidding, of course. He's great. I'm very… impressed."

Oro loved hearing that. He fidgeted some more, unable to contain his smile or his happiness at the comment. "Good, good. That's amazing!" And all the while they had this conversation, Mikalla just sat there, washing up in the torrent of their messy undulations, swept up and thrown down. *What do they want from me?*

Oro then turned toward Mikalla after more chatter and addressed him firmly. "So, Mikalla," he said, "do you know why you're here? Did Kitan say anything?" He waved his hand.

"All he said was that you wanted to see me?"

Oro took a sip of his drink. "Well, he was right. I *do* want to see you. Something important has occurred to me, something having to do with you."

"Me? Is it something serious? Did I do something wrong?"

"You didn't do anything wrong," Oro said, "but it *is* serious. Very serious. The life and death of the kingdom."

"What does that have to do with me?"

"That has to do with your future."

Kitan cleared his throat. He was not a part of the conversation, but possibly he wanted to be. Maybe he wanted to interject. His eyes darted back and forth, wishing and rooting for a certain outcome.

"You are The Conjurer's assistant, are you not?"

"I am."

"And so you know Gobi very well, as well as Yolia, correct?"

"I don't... I mean, I know them pretty well." Mikalla maintained his mental guard. He had no idea what was about to happen, but to mess it up would be tragic, possibly too tragic for his juvenile heart to bear.

He needed a means of either breaking out or breaking in, unlocking whatever Oro's plan was. "They're good people. The best people."

"Very well," Oro burped, "could you say you know a lot about the process of how they go about choosing The Conjurer?"

"I don't know. All I know is that Gobi was training to be Yolia's successor as The Conjurer when I got there." Mikalla felt the chilling eyes of Kitan melt holes in the tender side of his torso, scorching and freezing, but burning all the same. He had no idea what role Kitan played in this. He had no idea who Kitan even was. And now he seemed to dictate a portion of his future—possibly a large one.

"Well, did Yolia choose Gobi?"

"It would appear that way. I can't be sure about that though." The tides turned in Mikalla's head. Something told him to trust Oro. On balance, there was a fragment nagging at him, wondering and wondering, spinning on the same questions: *is it only information they want from me? Or is it more?* All the same, he was afraid to ask those questions for fear they'd come across as flippant or defensive. Worse yet, he could be let go by yet another opportunity of a lifetime. Here, he sat at the very top of the kingdom. Him, a low noble, barely more than a commoner of the masses, overlooked the many from a palatial window with space to spare. He couldn't let that go.

"Okay then," Oro said, sipping his drink again.

"If I may ask, what exactly am I here for?"

"Wanna get straight to the point?" Oro said, getting up from his chair. "That's fine. We'll get straight to the point. I want to make you The Conjurer."

Mikalla's heart leapt into another realm. Blissful blindness overtook his weary vision. A rainbow appeared where the sun used to be. Mikalla had a hope. Out of those simple words, a beautiful horizon had appeared. From somewhere impossible, some place miraculous and in the clouds, his chance had come. But it would not be an easy endeavor.

"Yes, I want to make you The Conjurer, and we are going to take every step toward getting you there." Oro faced him explicitly. "I like you, Mikalla." The first prince's face softened. His eyes watered before returning to their normal state, slightly pained, but all the way enthusiastic. "I like you. I trust you. And that means a lot. No one in that class gives me any respect. No one in general does."

"But everyone calls you by your title and kneels when you walk into the room," Mikalla said. Kitan nodded along with Mikalla as if he agreed with him. The two seemed puzzled at the notion that Oro didn't get respect. The first prince got *loads* of respect from everyone he came into contact with.

"Yes, and that's exactly the disrespectful, undignifying way I get treated every day!" Oro put his arms up, fists clenched in red and white balls. "I'm a human. I'm a human, and *you two*," pointing at them both, "are the only ones who seem to understand that. I have feelings, a beating heart, a mind that goes crazy. I'm a human, for God's sake. Thank you for respecting *me*." Oro began pacing again. This time quicker, sloppier. "We have a plan, and it involves you becoming The Conjurer."

Mikalla just gulped and sat back. The gravitas got to him, weighed him down with authority, and sent the situation spinning. He had not the power nor the grip on the reality of it all to say much of anything besides simple chops of language. "I want to be The Conjurer. I want to listen. I want to do this."

"Good, because you didn't have a choice." Oro said it seriously. He didn't smile. He didn't laugh. Mikalla understood he wasn't joking. "I believe in you."

This confidence in Mikalla from someone so esteemed and powerful, believing in him so surely, contented his soul. And then it hit Mikalla like a mad bull on a rampage—the steps they would have to take to make that happen.

Mikalla asked, "what do we have to do to make that happen? How do we make me The Conjurer?" He scanned between Kitan and the prince.

"We take out Gobi."

Kitan pitched in. "We need to neutralize him."

***

The rest of that conversation was planning and plotting. It had to do with Gobi, and Mikalla told them everything he knew about the boy, with eyes like hot coals and a rigid determination. Plotting and planning.

In Mikalla's head was a picture of triumph. He had a wonderful vision of Gobi sad, going down in defeat. He had to. Renewed hope made him smile; it made him see a future with a green horizon, something light and abundant toward status, and something like love. He had beauty in him after all, and he needed to get it out, scream it out if he had to. He would have to try. He would have to try to get his story out.

Chapter 17

Gobi had a crew of people gather around him. About a circle of six sat around, including Gobi. He sat with a stolid face and a clenched jaw, his legs crossed and confident. The other figures were cloaked in long and heavy dark material, so big and woolen that it obscured their faces. Gobi was the only one in the circle without a hood. They were in a basement of some sort, dimly lit apart from a candle here and a candle there and torches on the wall. The flames made their shadows dance—on the ground, on the walls and on the ceiling, sprawled even across the stern face of Gobi with vengeance in his eyes. Silence was all there was besides the echo of Gobi's voice, which sang the song of violence and blood.

"Hallowed members of the cloaks," Gobi started, "it is with pleasure and reverence that I receive your presence tonight. It is an honor, truly, to be surrounded by the backbone of Idaza, the hidden layer under the crust."

A voice sounded with sterile glee, demanding with only a word. Like a snake, he hissed. "Sacrifice."

"Yes, yes, of course." And Gobi reached into his robe, rustling to pull something out, something to please the cloaked figures that surrounded him. From within his pocket he pulled out a sack, filled to its brim, and barely sealed with an aching rope that appeared more like twine around a bag so tightly packed. It clanked on the table with a wave of silty objects rustling. The sack stuck to the table. All of the cloaks stared at it.

"Empty it," one said.

"Oh yes, of course." And Gobi yanked at the rope that enclosed it and emptied its contents onto the table. It contained a mountain of cacao beans and coins of the densest, most lustrous gold. Shimmering and clacking, a mound of pure value stored on the table, a transfer of wealth and power, a shadowy exchange in front of flickering torches. It all happened right there. Right in the moment, the royals bled a bit and the cloaks drank their wealth, their golden trust in them to get the job done. The secret backbone of Idaza's underworld surrounded Gobi.

"This is good. Now, what is the deed to be done?"

Gobi stopped putting the contents back inside of the bag and instead looked up at the cloaks, scanning and recrossing his legs. "I have a problem. A big problem. It's a threat to my safety, the kingdom, and my creativity, my dream."

"Get on with it."

"There is a boy, not much younger than me. His name is Mikalla."

"We know Mikalla."

An icy chill ran up Gobi's flesh and spine. *They know him? How could they know him?* His heart began to thump into his ears. "Do you... have you worked with him in the past?" Gobi waited in an anxious, fidgeting stew until they responded after a pause.

"No," one of them hissed. "Never. We watch him. We watch everyone worth watching. Including you, Gobi."

Something quelled inside of Gobi as he was able to continue his line of thought. He took a breath as he watched the shrouded faces of all of them fixate. Their grave expressions were hidden. The flames kept dancing. The torch light flickered on and on until Gobi spoke again. "Mikalla is threatening me and the position of The Conjurer in general. He is taking everything sacred about the role and perverting it. He's a monster. And he needs to be stopped."

"How is he doing this? He is the assistant to The Conjurer, is he not? How is he undermining you? You are still Yolia's apprentice."

Gobi gulped and stared at a flame adjacent to them. He shook a bit, transfixed on the orange-and-red being, the flicker that seemed more alive than any one person in that room. "He's...plotting. He's choosing to plot against me. I've heard him talking. I've seen the way he looks at me. He wants my spot, and he's close enough to get it. I need him to be in a position where he can't undermine me."

"And what position might that be?"

At this point, Gobi's face was wrapped in beads of sweat, succumbing to the heat of the torch-lit cellar. The room became a red inferno. "Dead. Not here anymore."

***

"And what do you have planned for the ceremony?" King Menizak asked. Eyes still sad. Face still solemn. It was as if he stared into the distance always, even while looking at a person. Sometimes, *especially* while looking at a person did he stare and gaze into a doll, a mere painting of himself, some sad rendering.

Yolia paced around. In contrast to the king's glum look, Yolia was lively. "Oh, it's going to be great. It's about the mythical story of Tehauxlochtl, the warrior slave. It's set in a distant kingdom. But the best part," Yolia said, sticking his index finger up and out into the air excitedly, "is that Gobi is going to be on the projection rock with me. Gobi is going to help me perform. We've been preparing immensely for it. Oh!

It's going to be grand!" Yolia nearly spun in excitement at his own news. The king just sat and nodded.

"Good. Good. That sounds like a good plan." But of course, nothing was good to the king then. Nothing was substantial, nothing was tangibly enjoyable anymore after the passing of his beloved son. "That'll be good for Gobi."

"Oh yeah, absolutely! Gobi will be enriched. It will be great."

The king cleared his throat and shifted a bit in his chair. "And what about Mikalla, the boy?"

"Well, I don't know, Your Majesty; what about him?"

"Mikalla—what part will he have in the ceremony?"

"None. He's an assistant but not quite ready to be put in front of the kingdom. He's not quite ready. He will be. He will be. Very, very talented."

"Why would you bring him in at all? He's only your assistant."

"Yes, but that doesn't preclude him from being a part of my crew. He has to express, Your Majesty. He has the same beast within him as me."

"You seem to speak glowingly about this boy. Tell me, why? Why such high praise for a low noble? Gobi tells me he's rather selfish and conceited, scared of the limelight and jealous of who has it all the same."

"He is selfish," Yolia said. "But so am I. And so is Gobi. There's vanity in creation. There's vanity in expression. My actions on the projection rock in front of the whole kingdom are imperious on their own. I'm selfish too."

The king seemed to have spat and laughed. "You always speak in poems, Yolia. You always have. But don't try and avoid the question. Don't avoid," the king looked into Yolia's eyes, venom in between the pair, "what we're talking about here." Something like an insidious knowing, rising and steeping and soaking on the floor and in the moist air between them, arose and lashed out and filled their nostrils and eyes while their brains tried to avoid it. They both knew, deep in the well of their own souls, what the other wanted, and they refused to let it go or have it surface. They refused to be the ones that gave in. But neither wanted to fight. Yolia's spirit was standoffish; the king was mired in grief that plagued his body and made him weak.

Yolia tried to grasp what they were dancing around. But he made the king do it instead. He wished for peace and protection. All Yolia wanted to do, in essence, and in the end, was to have someone truly great to succeed him, to tell his stories the way they knew how. He wished to rise above the influences from the outside and bring the people pieces of himself that added to a greater piece or person than himself. He wanted to project. And on those projections, he wanted to cast himself. Even the art was imperious, and in every story, a transgression, an overstep, a sales pitch to a naturally unwilling prospect.

But Yolia hated outside influence. "And what," Yolia said, "was it that we were talking about? What are you getting at exactly?"

The king gulped and had black recollections of his nephew decrying the boy, Mikalla, with vitriol and flame in his eye. The king just sat back and listened. Of course, Gobi was jealous. Of course, his ego was involved. But how could the king say no to his nephew after all he had lost in his family? The answer to the king was that familial bonds were priceless. In fact, those two things often went together. Priceless and irrational and beautiful. That was something the king had to look out for. Gobi was someone he had to vouch for. "We're talking about Mikalla," the king said. "And we're talking about your relationship with him. Why again do you need an assistant?"

Yolia began to get agitated. His demeanor changed. His face filled with storm clouds, gray and dark, the same as the thunder in his swirling gut. The eyes of fire set in his face, scintillating maggot pupils staring back at the king. His voice was not loud nor soft when he spoke but rather sharp and blunt. "I need an assistant for things outside people's knowledge. The general need for an assistant is different from The

Conjurer's need for an assistant. There are regular tasks I have him do, and then there are those which hit into the…mystical realm. A realm in which those that aren't The Conjurer may not understand. It's like asking why you need a court or why a bird of prey needs, well, *prey*."

"That didn't answer my question."

"Maybe some things can't be answered."

The king desperately hoped that this was not a provocation, a challenge. He wished he would not have a problem with Yolia. But he inevitably would. Because, mainly, Yolia did not listen and would not answer.

The King said slowly and deliberately, with the care of a parent's touch to her child, "are you defying me?"

But then Yolia did something unexpected. He bowed. "Of course not, my king, Your Highness. I would never think to defy you."

"Great. Then tell me, why do you need Mikalla? Because he has been causing me a lot of problems."

"Problems? How so?" Then it was Yolia's turn to be on the offense, to put the burden of proof onto the king. "What problems is Mikalla causing? This is news to me."

The king backpedaled verbally, thinking he'd made a mistake. "Well, people ask questions, Yolia, you know that. And when people hear that you just plucked a new assistant out of the high academy and he was a low noble, especially one unknown and not even districted to the high academy in the first place...well, people ask questions. They want to know why. And if the nobles are particularly rich or connected or close to the royal family, it gets back to me."

"Are any of these questions coming from *within* the royal family?"

"N-No," the king said. He never stuttered, not even when under pressure, and especially not during the heat of war. "Nothing from within the royal family."

"And so, Gobi hasn't asked anything? He hasn't brought anything up to you?"

"What are you getting at? Yeah, no, he hasn't said anything."

Yolia rubbed the broad side of his face with both hands, seemingly trying to wipe the crust of lies off. But he couldn't do that. Instead, to compensate, he asked a question. "So, Gobi does not have a problem with Mikalla? Because—"

"Not necessarily, no. It wouldn't appear so. But what were you going to say? I cut you off."

"I was saying that I sense some tension."

"Tension? Where?" The king asked.

"Between Mikalla and Gobi."

"How so?"

"Gobi doesn't like Mikalla. He may sense that he's some sort of threat; I don't know. But there's something there. I was wondering if you knew anything about that, considering Gobi's your nephew."

"I don't. I don't. It strikes me as odd, though—Gobi doesn't have anything to fear, does he?"

"About what?"

"About his spot being…taken."

"By Mikalla?"

"I don't know," The king said, "by anyone, I guess."

Yolia paused for a bit. He pictured in his head and his heart Gobi the boy, the teenager becoming the man. He pictured his future. Or at least, he tried to. Gobi's future was untold. And it hung in the balance of Yolia's whims and decision. He was meant to be the successor. But what did that mean anyway? The power of the story is equivalent to the power of the person. It was not to be taken lightly. Gobi was a scrap in the wind if he was not the successor. But who was he really? Yolia knew why the king was asking.

Of course, the king desperately wanted his nephew to become The Conjurer. "No," Yolia said, "there's no threat to his spot. Not unless he goes crazy or really screws up."

"Screw up? What would he have to do to screw it up?"

"I don't know. If he commits a serious crime. Does something he's not meant for before he's ready. If he interjected in front of a ceremony in an unwarranted way…that would kick him out of my program."

"*Your* program?"

"Yes. My program."

"But it's all mine."

"What is?" Yolia asked.

"Everything. The kingdom and the people in it." The king furrowed his brow, bending his face into something like a statue of authority, sheer will, imperiousness as a face, and a face as an infringement unto everything and anything in its way. "Everything that goes on is mine. Everything that breathes—their very breath is mine. Every decision made—their decisions are mine." The king's gravelly voice drew into a low growl, guttural and steep like a slippery hill but also broad like a mountain. "Everything under my nose is mine. And I stand on top of the highest hill."

"Of course," Yolia said. He nodded.

"And that means your decisions, too. They're mine."

"Then what say do I have?"

"Whatever I say, that's yours."

"Then what say do I have?"

"Irrelevant. I want to focus on Gobi. Please, tell me right now, for the sake of the kingdom and your own family and your stories and your life, tell me. Tell me Gobi has nothing to worry about."

"He has nothing to worry about."
"Good. You are excused."
"Thank you, your highness."

Chapter 18

All good royals train in self-defense.
The best royals train in death.

***

The studio was quiet. Hushed and deadened by a mood of black and hanging over the only three members within its dark bowels. It waned and washed over the soul's grime and quiet, desperate clambering to somewhere unknown. It was a cavern in the studio. Not homely. Not comely. Dark and quiet. Even the voices of the three individuals seemed to be hushed and solemn. Yolia had his jaw clenched and his legs crossed. He sat across from his assistant and his protégé. They both had solemn looks.

"We are a day out from the ceremony," Yolia said through the dense air of the studio, "and there are whispers in the corridors. Everywhere. I hear mumblings from places…places from around us. People are talking. There is much…tension. Tension everywhere. But most of all, there is tension within my studio. And I will not have tension. Out there, tension is okay. Tension is welcomed in the outside world. In fact, as artists, tension is what we feed off of. It is and can be great. But not here. Tension in my studio is disallowed. Here, we need cohesion. Here and in here, we need to be in flow, swimming by and through the unconscious. And so, in order to mitigate this tension I've been feeling as of late, Mikalla, I have to let you go."

Mikalla's heart was wrenched with mortal fear. The demons latched on. Stars streaked across his vision. What couldn't be true just came true. What couldn't happen just happened. There were no condolences for that which was truly broken. And this broke Mikalla.

"I'm sorry, Mikalla, but we don't need confusion and tension as we prepare for this ceremony tomorrow. You have been a good assistant to this point, and I would be happy to provide recommendations going forward." Yolia looked at the ground, forlorn, confused, just as Mikalla was. It was all confusing. "You're free to pack up your stuff now."

A cannon shot through his chest, bleeding and watching it bleed. That which he desired was out of reach. He lost connection with the most proper and powerful of the forces in the universe: purpose. He nearly stumbled out of his chair as he left to collect his bag and go far away. Far away from what he felt, far away from his pain. But he wouldn't be able to escape it.

Becoming The Conjurer

He could barely see, and he couldn't speak. The studio was a blur, a flash of obscurity, a kaleidoscopic, gray mess until he reached the outside. And his vision still blurred, only brighter, this time with colors vibrant of green and harsh yellow, sieging his seething eyes. His heart was in disarray, his soul, his being, his history, invalidated. Everything he wanted with a closed door in front, and now living a life of adjustment, of tumult and decay and regret.

He stumbled out of the studio. The sun-stroked wind attacked his skin and eyes, his soul and mind. He tried to process what had just happened, but there was nothing to process. In a matter of little time, he was praised, just to be brought down with a mighty crash. The only thought he had was to return to his parents. The only thing that could give him any cure or refuge. There was really no cure. He needed to see his parents, tell them what had happened, and cry. It was all he could do. A crushed soul was a crushed body. But he tried to slog, unable to move or do much of anything. The world spun around him. He re-lived—over and over—for an eternity, that one moment. Yolia's face, his words. Mikalla was nothing but a shadow, a skeleton, hollow and flat without his dream.

And then he pictured Gobi's face. Over and over again, he saw the smug look of a scared predator. A scheming werewolf always in human form, coiled and ready to strike. Sand in his eyes myopically, Mikalla saw his rival stare across at him as Yolia delivered the devastating news. *He had to be behind this. Gobi had to be behind this.* And the thought of that brought on a sharp pain, and it rang throughout his body, every nerve a knife, every vessel a vestige of suffering, weighing him down until he sunk into black, icy hell. Gobi's face, a smile of destruction. Mikalla could think of nothing but that. He yelled, but no one could hear. Or maybe that was in his mind too. Ecstatic pain, electrifying his body, preying upon every weakness which was everywhere and everything. Mikalla had no idea how much he needed to be The Conjurer's assistant. He had no idea how badly his soul yearned for freedom of expression until it was ripped from him.

But was the freedom of expression really ripped from him? *Am I really trapped?* He thought. *Was my expression gone, or just my position?* This thought gave a glimmer of hope, a tiny morsel in a sea of nothing but opaque wandering. *I could be alone and express myself. I could be with no one, yet I could still be myself.*

***

While home, he told his parents what had happened. They grieved his loss and were deeply saddened by his rejection. He then asked to be alone.

Becoming The Conjurer

That's what he was now, anyway—alone. All he wanted to do and all he did was walk upstairs and shut the door to his room. He closed the shutters and shades. Welcoming in darkness, he wore it like a cape. He lit all the flames and pulled out a parchment. Taking a pen while feeling the heat of the whispering fire, he got to work. He wrote down a sentence, an urge from the gods. He managed to wrangle another sentence onto the page. He put word after word, a feeling, a flame. And he continued to write. He wrote out his disgust. He wrote out the lonely, lonely feeling in his gut and smacked it, plastered it onto the page. He wrote the symphony of the solace of solitude, all while calculating ways of getting out of his misery. But the misery always came back, every second, rearing its head and reminding him why he deserved his wretched and lonely fate. That he would always be alone. And the misery only made his writing more intense. He tried to picture the waves of pain in his head, realize their impact, and put a face to them. *Gobi.* But he ran thoroughly away from the face. He pictured it less and then not at all. He couldn't face reality, the careful craftsman behind his demise.

And he continued to write and scrawl out his pain on paper. It went on and on, a drivel of ink from the well of his soul. He felt the words weren't getting any better, but he pushed on through, through to a place of exhausted effort, the pen drying out every so often and needing more fuel to lay out his misery on the page.

Separated. Let go. Rejected. Fired. Me, a reject. Me, outsmarted, outdone, out-hustled by some snob.

And then Gobi's face twisted again into the cavity of his tired mind. He shuddered and dropped the pen. Visceral agony painted his face. Bleeding from every orifice, the nectar of pure pain. Pure deprivation. He tried to spill it onto the page, but the most potent substance was a tear that stroked his cheek and then the parchment, blurring and splotching some places where he'd written.

It's hopeless.

He looked for solace, something to move him. He found nothing amidst the words. He backed up and away from his chair. He snatched the parchment from his desk and gulped, and then read the words he wrote on the page. They were garbage. They were terrible words, a terrible string that emoted nothing. He hated those words just as he'd hated himself.

He looked at the page some more, searching for an answer. Searching for something to say it'd be alright in the end. But his words were terrible, and his posture stooped to reflect the defeat he saw in every stroke of the pen. He was too young to yearn for non-existence. He felt nothing and everything, and still, with every beat, a stolid lump of aching flesh, waiting to be beaten on again by his remorseful heart.

Though there was no end to his pain, he searched for one anyway. And he wrote some more and then stared at the flame in front of his nose, straddling his eyes and the air. It danced. A lone jewel, eager to be put out, its whole life just a mass of consumption of the air afforded it. *Even the stupid flame is hopeless, just like me. Why did Gobi have to do this? Why was I even born? This whole situation is out of my hands.*

And while in his shaking hands, the parchment continued to be stroked by tears, tears falling like lanterns, then exploding off into every scintillating direction when hitting the marked canvas. He was someone, and that was the problem. Because he wanted to be nothing. Why was he put here just to feel the pang of deprivation so deeply? There had to be a reason? There had to be an answer for suffering, something to make it worth it. *Gods, why? Why have you put me here? Am I just a stepping stone for snakes?*

Drenched in the pitiful reek of tears, Mikalla went to sleep. It was not restful. It was not sound. It had not a great effect nor a single moment of peace. His heart's flame flickered and waned to the wasteland. His body, without any further effort or resistance, would be given up to the stars assuming his soul had died.

But on that night, it hadn't yet died. The flare of his heart hadn't given out—not yet, not like that. And as long as there was still a spark, there would be a fight, a chance to reach, if only once more, toward the heavens from a body of dust and flesh.

But for Mikalla, there was still a chance. For Mikalla, there was still hope.

Chapter 19

"I know. This is an outrage." Prince Oro stood looking out from the palace's grand balcony. He looked out toward the city. It hummed from the great distance between its commons and the enraged look the prince wore.

"And so the question is, what to do." Kitan paced about.

"Goddamn it. Goddamn it all!" The prince slammed his fist against the railing with force. "I knew this kid Gobi would be a problem. I knew he would be. And we waited." The prince seethed in an angry trance. He turned toward Kitan. "Why did we wait?"

Kitan was taken aback. A miscalculation. This was his time. This was his chance. His wildest dream, his vision, was coming true before his eyes. He dined among the elites after being a quasi-slave. An orphan, adopted by luxury. And he waited too long. To strike. To do much of anything. His strategy did not pay off.

Oro had a flash of insight, a secret folk-tale that was passed around among the royal children. It was a myth untold to commoners and even the rest of the nobility, too poor or not well-connected enough to be close to the royals. This folk-tale was a mere whisper among palatial halls. It could just have been an empty story and just that: a story. But he had to give it a chance. It was their last hope.

Oro looked at Kitan. "There is a story told to children of the royal family. It's a gruesome one. It always scared me as a kid. But we have to give it a shot.

Kitan perked up.

And the prince began to explain all about the mythic royal folk-tale of a secret, underground society of hooded men, killers, willing to do anything for the right price. They were accessible only to royals who knew where to look or who to ask. They were dawned in dark cloaks and willing only to meet in the dark, dimly lit cellars. Oro recited a poem to Kitan. It was the folktale's main saying.

Beneath you,
Around you,
Stalking all the time—
The shadows in the night
Seek to serve you
For the right price.

"They'll do anything?" Kitan asked. His eyes lit up. "What do we pay them with?"

"Anything and more," Oro said, "but how the hell do we know who to ask? Or how to ask, for that matter? I can pay for them. I have enough."

"We'll figure it out."

"And how to do that?"

"Well, have you asked your father?"

Oro winced at the thought. He knew very well his father would suspect him of something nefarious, something unclean, and would be very curious to know why he wanted to meet with the men with masks. *But what would he say? How would he respond?*

"I haven't, but something tells me that'd be dangerous. It could give us up."

"Maybe," Kitan said, "but who else would know about the men in masks? Who else would have access to them? The king would be a sure bet to this society. Surely he knows, and few others do."

Oro stood thinking. His head is in the clouds. He wandered the space in his head, searching for an answer. He didn't know, besides his parents, who would be appropriate to ask for this.

They deliberated. Continuing to search for a sign would propel them. And for the longest time on that balcony, as the sun turned to the moon, nothing came to them. Few answers sprouted among a forest of indecision, dead ends, and roadblocks.

Finally, they came upon the inevitable.

"I'll ask my father," Oro said, "and I'll make something up. What should I say, though?"

Kitan put his hand to his bony chin.

"It needs to be something to enrich him, the king. Something to help further his own agenda. Then he'll help you. Maybe say you need to talk to the men in masks to help the king spy on a neighboring city. Anyone. Just pick one."

"Would that work? You think he'd really buy that?"

"We must try."

***

The king looked at a painting. His face was long. His eyes were drawn like tattered shades. A single well of feeling amassed in the corner of his eye. The painting depicted his son. It was large, tall, and grand, much like his memory in the heart of the kingdom and its sad ruler. He shed a tear. He shed a tear for his son. He shed a tear for his family. He shed a tear for the grave that robbed him of his joy, his son. Menizak The Younger was a warrior, just like Menizak The Older. He was brave and calm under pressure, defiant in the face of danger.

At a noise, the king turned around to face the incoming footsteps of his other son, his younger one. Oro walked in. He had the face of someone asking for something. It was like he wore a question mark on his face, waiting, watching, searching for the answer he wanted. The king instinctively knew this look on his son's face. He knew that he wanted something. He just didn't know what exactly his son wanted. But there was hope, a glimmer that gave the king a warm feeling, seeing his last son with determination. Oro had a willful stride walking into his father's throne room, something he thought he'd never see from the boy. But the boy was changing right before his father's eyes.

"Father."

"Son," the king said, face both stern and soft, posture sinking, "what would you like?"

"I have a question, father, but also a favor to ask."

"And what is that?"

"Well," Oro started, "I'm getting older now, I'm growing, I'm getting more... independent. With that said," Oro took a breath, a deep inhale as he watched the world stop moving around him, "my favor is this: you don't ask anything about my next question."

The king crossed his arms. Interested, he bent his powerful, sullen brow and pursed his lips in thought. The air was dense between the two. There was nothing the king could say that could deter Oro. He was determined, and his father was deflated, weak, hollowed out with black grief, plaque eating away at his insides, making an energetic way for the next turbulent chapter of the kingdom.

The king thought some more about Oro's proposition. It was so sudden. It was decisive. *Maybe he is growing up. Maybe there is a warrior inside him, after all. Maybe. Maybe…there is hope with the kingdom in his hands.* The king decided to run with Oro's proposition after more staring and grinding his teeth. He took a deep breath. "Okay, son." Another deep breath from and within and through his hollow guts. "I'll accept that. I can do that. No questions. Now, what is it you need, prince?"

He called me prince, Oro thought excitedly. "Father, I only come with one request."

"And that is what?"

"I want to meet the men in masks. I need to have a meeting with them."

The king was taken aback, yet he kept his face the same, kept the same, slinking posture. He scratched his head. "What do you know about them?"

"I know that I needed to ask about them, and I figured you were the one to go to."

"You were right about that."

***

Becoming The Conjurer

Mikalla was on a walk. It was the only time he found any solace in anything after being let go as Yolia's assistant. He struggled in school at that point. He made no assignments, his mind a prison in which he could not break out. His vision on the walk and, in general, was like looking through a layer of gray dust out at the gray world.

But from the shadows and unseen nooks of the Inner Gardens, he was being watched carefully, surveyed clearly, and stalked perfectly from keen eyes both close and far away.

And still buried within Mikalla was a pain that urged to come out was a flame to illuminate the murals on the walls of the labyrinth of life. Still within him was the ancient, age-old drama, the poignance of the human capacity for struggle and beyond. The triumph of the human will burst at his seams, flooding every nook in his soul, crushing him with its giant inertia until he found an audience or an outlet. And it still crushed him that, because of Gobi, he was forever cast away from his audience, his expression, unable to even bring to a parchment page what he was feeling.

With every step came a new question; every landing of his foot, an answer deprived of its being. Only pain from this point on.
And yet, somehow, on his walk, he saw a familiar figure. His insides quaked with indecision, uncertainty,

excitement, and finally, with the threat of grave danger—all at once, an avalanche. It was Kitan. Tall and slender and fixed with a determined gaze toward Mikalla, who walked his way then.

"Mikalla, how are you?" They walked toward one another. Each felt a tension in the morose air, something afoot or static energy everywhere stinging and tasting the skin. "It's grand to see you."

They led Mikalla back to Oro's quarters.

Dusk began to creep through the window. Twilight encroached with wiry fingers, grasping at the three in the room.

It was Kitan that broke the desperate silence in the giant room. His voice collided with the colossal pillars and the grand mural on the ceiling.

"Mikalla, we're going to kill Gobi."

Chapter 20

The young prince had everything he needed. He had the approval and information from his father. He had the strategy from his adviser. He had the motive from Mikalla. He had to get this done. It was the only way to secure his complete future on the throne. An uncontrolled Conjurer meant uncontrolled results. A Conjurer who had his own plan meant leaving the king out of it. Just as Gobi could oust Mikalla through his own will, Oro would have to exert his own doubly as hard as he descended into the deep bowels of the Inner Gardens. The path he took was from within the royal palace itself.

A set of stairs grew dingier and dirtier with every step. The dust seemed to wallow. The railing seemed to cry and creak and moan. The flames on the wall shrieked. Oro looked down. There were so many to climb. The darkness peered back at him. The giant masses of white cobwebs laughed at him. He took a deep breath. He had no songs in his head, no poems to recite that could quell his vicious nerves tingling like the teetering flames around him, black and blue from the dust of ages past.

Nick Oliveri

The closer Oro got to the deepest bowels of the inner cave, the faster his heart ran and boomed in his ears. The darker the stairway got, the more he saw in his own mind's eye. He saw scenes of destruction, of killing and knifing. Depictions of death emblazoned the dark of his eyes. The fear in him dug its black tentacles into the soul, the psyche, the senses, wrapping and wringing, rapping and ringing, in his ears and through his heaving pores like the handles of twiglike oars in the fanged mouth of a blackened swirling storm. It was him and only him then, stepping into the depths.

The darkness soon blanketed him. He could hear howling, yet there were no sounds. He could see demons dancing, and yet his eyes reflected and reported nothing. He was there, there in the cave, the depth, the sanctum where the shadows lived, where the men in masks made their home. He had on him jewels to satisfy a lifetime of splendor and lust and bottomless envy. Where the shadows spent this money, he had no idea.

"Who goes there?"

Oro jumped and nearly fell at the voice. And with sudden determination, it was as if the wind itself breezed life into the torches of the room. There, in the middle of the room of torches, was a table. Beside it stood a man, or, presumably, a man, in a large cloak, too large to see under or through.

And then Oro thought about his answer. He spat it out as quickly as it had come to him. "It is I, Oro. The first Prince of Idaza."

"And why do you come?"

"I come on account of business. I seek…a transaction."

"You are unannounced. Your arrival is unexpected."

Oro thought about it. And his life came through his mind like a caravan passing, and his fears showed their faces one by one. He shivered and huddled and shrugged his shoulders. He felt like turning around. *What if they don't accept the task? What if they reject me? What if they kill me? What if they rob me? What recourse do I have against the shadows?*

"Yeah, maybe," Oro said, "I'm sorry."

And more of the masks came out from the shadows. More figures from beyond the torched room emerged as if from the dust.

"Your apology can only be accepted under certain circumstances…move the bag this way."

Oro pushed the sack across the table. All was still and silent in the dank cavern beside the clinking of the coins in the bag. It was enough for a king's ransom. Precious jewels and royal heirlooms sat in that bag. Oro wondered what the shadow did with all that money, who they were, and even what they influenced by the number of jewels they were given. *Maybe they rule the whole city, and no one knows....*

The cloaked figures all huddled around the sack—examining the gold. Clinking. Jingling. Pieces fell and were then gripped in the bony fingers of the hands of the members.

Oro just sat and stared, drenched in sweat. He wiped his wet brow with a wet arm, and that only made him more slippery. But finally, an answer came from a screechy voice.

"What do you want?"

Oro gulped. "I- I want…."

And as Oro spoke, his mind melted from the heat of his swirling surroundings. *I need a drink,* he thought.

"You may leave if you intend to waste our time."

"No, no, that's not my intention—trust me. I do want something in exchange."

"What is it?"

"I want you to kill Gobi, The Conjurer's apprentice."

The room fell silent. But really, they came out as a whisper and still hushed the cavern and the many masked beings before him.

They would go on to become possibly the greatest words the kingdom had ever heard.

What interested Oro was that the masks all seemed confused, not knowing what to do or say next.

Becoming The Conjurer

They just looked at one another. They were thinking. But Oro's mind was blank, and their minds were riddled with conundrums.

And then one of them eyed the bag of gold and jewels on the table and looked at the young, plump prince one more time. "It will be done, my lord. Now, return upstairs as quickly as you came down."

Nick Oliveri

Chapter 21

The day of the ceremony had arrived. Long awaited and with many motivations, all interweaving to make for a great show of parity and violence.

But it was not in the palace or the commons where the most impact would be had. No house nor stadium could control the city quite like what was directly below it.

The underground, in the shadows of the kingdom's light, lurked the decision-makers that held the balance of the ceremony and the king's crown in the tips of their hands.

One of them spoke up amidst the rushing feet, scattering all around as if they all intended to pace in line with one another.

They were the masked men, and they stood in disarray.

They laid both bounties on the table in a big pile of gold and shining blues and greens.

"Everyone just stand back."

"Has this ever happened before?"

"No. We've never faced this before. Two competing assassination requests. It's unprecedented."

"Well, we got orders from the prince. Plus, if you add it up, he gave us a higher price. We can't upset the prince. Gobi is merely a blue-blooded nobleman. We have to kill Gobi."

Murmurs rose and dissipated throughout the cavern. Nods of agreement came from many of the cloaks.

"There is something you may not know yet—something we have to discuss today."

Everyone turned toward the elder. "What's that?"

"It's not the prince we have to worry about." The room silenced. "It's the king."

Breaking the silence, someone spoke up from the back of the cavern, somewhere away from the table. "What do you mean by that?"

"The king is backing Gobi. If Gobi ends up dead, the king would know who and…possibly why…."

"So what do we do? Just kill some lower noble boy with nothing to offer us or influence the community at all? Both the king and prince are important."

"Well, what if we turned King Menizak against Prince Oro?"

"How?"

"We must strategize about how to do this. We may need to go to the war room."

"The war room it is." The elder pointed to one of the cloaked figures. "Stand guard in case a royal comes down to meet with us. Just tell them, 'we are working on something vital to the survival of the kingdom.' Okay?"

"Okay."

The room filtered out and emptied until there was just one figure left. The cavern grew quiet as the footsteps hushed into the air.

All was dark save for a few candles guarding the pile of gold and jewels out in the open.

A young, nasally voice poked through the silence. "You ever wonder what you could do with that money on the table? I mean, that amount—it's gargantuan. It could change your life. Think about—"

"Show yourself! Who goes there?"

The room stayed empty until the person that matched the voice emerged from the darkness into the flickering candlelight. He wore a white-and-black mask that formed a ghoulish face.

"Show your face, boy. I don't care if you're a royal."

"You could swipe a quarter of this bounty and live in luxury in another kingdom for the rest of your life."

Silence split the two for a while. Staring—neither one was able to discern the other's identity. A silent standoff.

"I'm going to call the elder and the rest of them if you take one step closer." The figure took one step backward, switching his glances between the pile of gold and the masked kid near the stairs.

Slowly stepping.

The cloaked figure turned to yell toward the war room.

But it was too late. All that came from his mouth was a grunt as a shank of clean obsidian dirtied itself on cloth and flesh embedded in the back of the figure.

Many stabbings later, the kid stepped over the silent pool of blood and hopped to the table of gold. Shoving as much of it as his arms and garments would carry. It clinked and jingled as he heard voices from deeper in the cavern.

The underground's golden bounty was robbed by a boy in a mask as he ran as fast as he could back up the stairs, hurrying and tiptoeing. He slipped by everyone and made off with gold, money, and jewels.

The boy escaped with everything. That boy's name was Kitan.

***

Above the stairs and into the light, Kitan had to swindle past guards and royals walking into the palace with a whole treasure trove in his arms. But he was up for the challenge. He heard footsteps, but his heart didn't race. His head just swiveled, and his eyes searched for ways out. He always did see many ways forward, and even in the balance of life and death, his hands didn't shake the gold, nor did his knees wobble at the sight of a guard.

This was an offense worthy only of the death penalty. Kitan was no stranger to the rules. What he wasn't accustomed to, however, was breaking them.

***

Gobi gazed into his mirror. He felt comfortable in front of the obsidian sheet, reflecting back an image true only to him—himself. He put on his glittering robe with accents all over and turned around, glancing from side to side, checking his angles. He took one last look in the mirror and grimaced, a menacing smile. Pain and joy, pride dominating his brow. Eyes like a tiger's. He was ready, and with Mikalla out of the way, he was finally comfortable. He smirked as he walked out of his vast room toward the ceremony stage.

He thought of one thing on his trip there: the projection flame, burning the oil, eating the air, creating life.

A certain type of greed consumed him like a fire.

Chapter 22

"Mikalla! It's time to go to the ceremony." His parents yelled up the stairs.

But Mikalla wasn't in Idaza. Mikalla's mind and heart were chained in hell, scared of the world. He wondered what his life amounted to and asked himself—over and over again—the biggest questions that life had to offer as his mother called from down the stairs. He couldn't take it.

"What! What could be so important about a ceremony?" He yelled down to his parents, and maybe, in a way, he yelled that to the world. He yelled at Yolia and Gobi. He yelled at Idaza and its tradition. Everything.

So what if Gobi dies? Maybe he's the lucky one....

And as Mikalla turned around, he jumped at the sight of his father, stern and staring down at him.

"Mikalla," he said, "you don't mean this. I know you don't." His voice was deep and stern. "You need to go."

Mikalla looked away from his father. *These stories just come from people. Just like you and me, Dad. That's it. They're manufactured and done selfishly, and they get all the influence. And what do I get? What do the commoners get? They get controlled. I get controlled. It's all about control. Well, guess what? I'd rather die than be controlled!*

Mikalla's face burned bright red. He then faced his father, and they locked eyes. All went blank as he uttered his next words.

His father replied.

Mikalla fired back.

His dad's face went cold.

Mikalla gulped and replied again. "Fine." Mikalla was forced into going. Even though Mikalla had to be there, it didn't mean he had to listen or engage with anything. He didn't have to take in the story or be swept up in the plot. He didn't have to care about the characters or even look at the images on the rock. To him, the shadows were just illusions. To Mikalla, the projections were just that: projections. They were flat and fake and stolid. All on a cold rock.

Mikalla and his family walked toward Mount Chuxat for the ceremony. Mikalla dragged his feet yet continued all the same. *This is my life,* he thought.

***

But right beneath his sandals was an uprising, a violent riot of cloaks and daggers. Figures scrambled while looking at the table, missing the only thing they were loyal to. All that was left was a single shining coin in the middle of the table where a mound of riches once stood. Shrieks broke the silence, and daggers rose out from cloth. Metal met flesh, and red ran all over the floor. Footsteps sank in puddles. Bodies dropped.

Grunts and yelps littered the halls of the underground. Gasps turned to echoes, and blindness ensued. A storm brewed and sank the figures in pellets of blood.

The masks and cloaks and dark figures of the underground were no more but rather just a pile, a house of straw atop an empty sheet. And the slightest tiff of wind knocked it down and blew it all away.

The single gold coin represented the lone survivor sitting in the darkness, removing his hood that revealed a beard breathing hard. He clutched his side and gasped, and looked all around. His eyes had yet to adjust to the underground's harsh blackness. The torches didn't seem to do the trick, as they only illuminated small splotches of blood, making them dance despite the lack of movement everywhere.

He shut his eyes and grimaced in the dark underground. The belly of the city swallowed him whole.

The luster of the coin shone too bright for their eyes and blinded them despite being in the dark. And then the light from the upstairs closed down on the cavern.

***

Above the cavern and death of the cloaked figures, Mikalla continued to walk alongside his family toward the ceremony. He dragged his sandals with every step. Waiting, wanting for something to happen.

But nothing came. Nothing happened. His hopes were all in vain as he continued on, head hung low. Memories of being in the studio with Gobi and Yolia bit at him. And he couldn't (nor wouldn't) be consoled by the stories of someone who rejected him.

There were buildings and people buzzing all around him as the whole city walked in a careful and synchronized stride. But all Mikalla could see or think of was Gobi's face. Smirking or staring. Always keeping watch and lifting the tendrils of Mikalla's inner stress strings tighter, tighter yet until they snapped. And then all he could see were stars.

***

Oro sat alongside his father's cold shoulder and the rest of the royal family, aside from Gobi, who, with

Becoming The Conjurer

Yolia and the rest of the ceremony crew, set up while hidden away behind the projection rock.

The sun's purple fringes showed through sparse gray clouds as dusk reared its head once again. Oro's mind spun, and his face screwed up with tension, tightened mind, and sweaty palms. *What's going to happen? Is Gobi really going to die before this ceremony? What if they just took my money and ran off with it? I wonder what Mikalla's feeling right now.... And where's Kitan?*

***

Kitan sidled along the outside wall of the palace. Shifting his eyes, tuning his ears to any possible movement. But it seemed as though most people besides the guards left the palace for the ceremony.

He still held the pile of treasure in his garments and arms and tried not to drop a single coin or jewel. The gold in his hands felt like the weight of the world.

And visions of possibilities and leverage danced in his head. He watched the palace as he left it. Turning to look, he thought, *this could be mine. This could all be mine.*

And eventually, he eluded the guards and the passersby with arms still full of cash and gold. The Inner Gardens were largely empty. Kitan was finally alone, swiveling his head and looking for a place to hide, to grow, or to leverage his newfound fortune. Those coins could have gone anywhere, and, eventually, they would go everywhere. He made it back to his shanty with a broom in one corner and a simple desk of crippled wood. He looked at the city he built with his mind, materialized of wood and stone and clay. It loosely resembled the kingdom of Idaza but had additions of tracks and wire that connected street markets and people and homes. It was Idaza but easier. It was Idaza but quicker. It was Idaza but better connected. And Kitan looked down at the model of the better of Idaza. He laid the mound of riches in the corner of the hut save for one coin. He dropped the coin in the middle of the model and watched it gleam amidst the clay and wood. A true jewel rose from a swamp, it looked like.

  He picked up the shining coin and stared at his own reflection. Brightly, a narrow face with snake-like eyes shone even in the dark.

  Questions arose:
Where will I find the engineers?
How will I hide this from Oro?
Where are our best scientists?
What could go wrong? And what would be the punishment?
How will I navigate through the cracks of each government, slowly enticing them to fall into my vision?

Becoming The Conjurer

But Kitan traipsed toward and against the dusty wall and slowly slid down its side until he sat in the dust and dirt. His garments grew filthier by the second. Dust clouds bustled beside him, rolling onto the model on the desk like a storm.

The boy looked at it. And then he looked back at the lone broom in the corner, splintered, wooden, futile. He no longer identified with his work or his broom, his status, or his room. And in due time, the advancement he needed would surely come true.

The gears of the city would surely crush him if he didn't deploy his funds; he had to move his money around and weaponize it just as the soldiers wielded spears.

His eyes grew a fearsome shade of yellow as the sky set down its purple blanket for the night, over the hills, underneath the puncturing stars. He fashioned most of his ratty garments into a large sack in which to hold his treasure. He hoped the garments would conceal the devastating gleam it showed when the light hit it—all of the coins and jewels in all their devious glory, their envy-inciting, violent luster.

But it wouldn't be an overnight process. He stayed in his house that night—away from the ceremony and away from everyone—writing in the dirt and shivering in the cold.

Nick Oliveri

***

The whirr of the crowd far away vibrated the box seats of the royal seating. Jani sat there as well, just a seat down from the Prince. Jani always needed, yearned for, thirsted for, lusted for, the closest seat to power. She kept watch of all the nobles and the king and the priests, the general, and the rest of the extended royal family.

A brown-haired hawk, not swooping, not preening. She watched from sizzling, steaming eyes waiting for movement and then reveling in its proximity. But still wanting more, listening to the quake of its never-sated stomach. A machine and an animal. She was the most elegant ugly beast. Never gnashing, always watching. Hunger was an end, not a driver, but rather, the goal itself. Yes, Jani displayed hunger in her eyes and thirst in her beaten soul. Thin and dark-eyed, sonsie and long with high cheekbones, brows perfectly matched, emanating the sweetest seductive scent to anyone, everyone. Jeweled-soft skin, big and full lips below beautiful pouting eyes. She was perfect among the perfect and spotless royals. A general among the generals, war-like in a city full of soldiers—Jani sat daintily with her legs crossed under a thin smile. She tapped the royal next to her to get Oro's attention.

"Hey cousin, are you excited for it to start?"

But Oro didn't look so good. Jani saw on his face wrinkles of dread despite his youth. She saw a boy, a young prince, aged with concern.

"Yep."

"Is there something wrong?"

"No. Why?"

"Because, Oro, you're not smiling and bouncing around for the ceremony like you usually do. What's wrong?"

"Nothing. I'm excited." And then he turned away.

This left Jani's gut trembling and on fire, weighted down at the sight of the back of Oro's head. Dejected.

Oro looked on with steady eyes and quivering feet. *What the hell's going to happen to Gobi? Where's Yolia? What story are we getting tonight? Will we even get a story? What if I get found out? Would they ever give me the death penalty?*

But as Oro's mind melded with a dark glob of thoughts, the sound of drums from a faraway place—the projection rock—began to electrify the dark air of the night. Booming. Beating. Sounds of angst and power sniping through the air. It burned the tinges of each person's hair throughout the ceremony. It shattered the wind and broke the barrier between every human in the entire stadium.

And in the dark, a light grew strong as a flame wound up its body and unleashed a holy presence that rained down on the people of Idaza. So many watchful ears. Anticipating. The colossal ceremonial blaze met the darkness and set the stadium on fire. Every face in the crowd alit with hope and fervor and madness.

Drums smashed the air and enchanted the ears of the entire city. Mikalla shifted and shivered in the crowd. He just wanted to be asleep or away from this mess. He tried to shove his envy aside or bury it deep away from his other feelings. He couldn't. He felt like crying or running or throwing something. He felt like inciting a riot or watching the ceremonial flame burn and blaze so ferociously that it swallowed everyone whole. *Look around,* he thought. *I'm going to be one of them. My entire life, I'm going to be working for this. I'm going to be feeding this. My blood is going to be donated to a larger cause, subject to the whims of an arbitrary regime. Something ignorant and blind. I just can't stand for it.* And yet, as everybody stood, he had to as well. He had to stand for it and take it and be one with it. It all made him sick.

And then a voice boomed. Mikalla could tell who it was right away.

"People of Idaza!" Yolia's figure appeared to be the size of the mountain in front of the whole city to see. His voice boomed and bashed through the air.

And he told a story of betrayal. Two boys. The same motive. They shifted and maneuvered against one another, but the other was better connected and better skilled at the craft of stabbing those in the back he needed to. But was there a moral to the story?

Mikalla looked around at the hundreds of thousands of people in the stands, tantalized by the story. The story of him. The story of his demise. It made him squirm in his seat and want to shout. He had a fit and yet said nothing. He looked at his parents; they were entranced too. In awe, eyes wide shut with mouths gaped open. He looked at the rest of the crowd with the same reaction—dumbfounded. There was no one who was not completely under the spell of The Conjurer.

But there was something toward the end of the story—something Mikalla couldn't deny. He heard Yolia's voice, and it was tinged with a touch of sadness. Something like remorse (or so Mikalla thought) stroked the night-dark air of the ceremony.

He spoke. Not as part of the story but *about* the story. A reflection on the story. He described, for the entire city, the entire *kingdom*, the pain and anger involved. Yolia bared *Mikalla's* soul in front of everyone. They were changed because of Yolia's words.

He spoke some more.

"And the boy was down and crippled, possibly for life!" The figure on the projection rock seemed to grow while its arms stretched to the sky, so its body made a dramatic 'V.' A triumphant man stood atop the projection rock with a sad story to tell.

"For every tear shed in the darkness, a lifetime of hurt. For each night, he closed his eyes, a displacement forever. And a displaced boy he was. Alone in the world. Stuck in the middle of the tears and agility, aggression, and sadness. He no longer jumped out of bed in the morning, for his feet dragged, and his heart frothed with indignation. This was a boy, broken by the onslaught of life." And displayed on the projection rock was a boy just like him, slouched with a head hung over his chest, trudging along and staring at the dirty ground. *A boy just like me,* Mikalla thought.

And as he watched along with the rest of the city, he felt the warmth of Yolia's voice, the sincerity laced in every stroke of his tone. It calmed him. Mikalla felt somehow comforted by Yolia's story and the way he told it. He felt that the entire kingdom had sympathized with him. He watched, entranced, as his dreams turned to a concrete state, and he swayed his head and eyes and heart with the rest of the crowd.

Yolia hummed from the heights. The crowd repeated and echoed the same until the whole mountain shook. And Mikalla took this well. And the stands vibrated as well. And the whole of the city became one within Yolia's grasp. Bracing them for certainties not privy to them.

The entire city would walk willingly into an alligator trap if Yolia led them there.

But things were not as cohesive on the projection rock as they were in the crowd.

***

Gobi turned around toward the drummers. "Harder! More! Quicker! Faster!" As Yolia spoke to the people, he quickly reared his head back at Gobi. He heard his commands and saw a flash of his face by the flicker of the giant flame. The boy looked crazed. The boy looked feral and ambitious—a combination that churned Yolia's gut as he turned back around to speak to the people. *What am I going to do with that boy*?

But Yolia kept on speaking to the public and only grimaced once after looking back at Gobi. *He just wants to be a part of the ceremony,* he thought to himself, coaxing his own mind into a belief about Gobi's good nature. But was his nature good? Who really was Gobi? *Who really is that boy*?

All while giving a speech on the trials of treachery and lust for power, he thought of Gobi and his eyes and his voice. The outlines of his brow to his pointed chin added up to something hard-driving and powerful. He had eyes that narrowed when he smiled.

And for the first time during a ceremony, Yolia shuddered and fell out of his free-flowing rhythm. It might have shown on the projection rock. It might have shown in the crowd, on the many faces of the awed people.

It all came to him.

It all fell onto his colossal and shadowed shoulders in that instant. The whole of the conflict. Everything. *Mikalla is the rightful successor. But there's nothing I can do about the king's opinion. Or the fact that Mikalla is the lowly son of clerks, barely a noble himself. But what to do?*

From the grand height of the projection rock, Yolia stared down at the masses. A massive swath of Influence's weapon. The price for the heart and mind of this collective people is priceless. *There are no riches that would be worth trading this for,* Yolia thought. As he stood above them, so he stood above the world and all its beasts and metal, all its people and petty problems.

And what would he do? What would he do with his influence, his might that rivaled all the kings of the world? He thought. He thought in a flash while the world seemingly crumbled around him. He had no control yet held the weight of the city in his palm.

And while he stood in front of the crowd with his arms held high, he took a breath and retreated one step. He backed away and to the side, fading and, with it, the voices of the crowd. All faded. All went silent, waning to a hush that sounded so loud it could shake the mountain. Nothing crept, moved, or shook. The wildly silent stadium reflected the contemplative mind of Yolia. There was little he felt he could do, and yet he held all the power in the world—unlimited potential to keep it or ruin it. All the world's money could not buy Yolia's influence at that moment.

And then he gave it up. He forfeited his unbridled power…to Gobi, the yeller, the untamed boy who had a heart and a mind that worked with ridiculous precision. But he wasn't ready for what was about to happen.

Yolia continued to step away from the podium and to the side of the flame so his image was distorted. But to replace his figure was a larger one, one that blazed and shook the waking crowd. It was Gobi, and all he did was step forward as Yolia waved him in front of the flame as soon as he finished his story.

As a colossal shadow, Gobi was a lone giant, upright and confident. But on his face was smeared a look of disdain and mortal shock. He turned back toward Yolia. Both the boy and the man, The Conjurer and the apprentice stood there and stared at one another. Gobi over his thin shoulder and Yolia straight ahead—staring.

Yolia had a stolid look with a glint in his eyes, the slightest grimace on his lips and on his brow. Gobi held nothing but fear—on his face, his thin frame, and everywhere else in his soul that could carry.

Yolia motioned him forward. As Gobi stepped away from the flame toward the edge of the platform and for the rest of his life, he gulped the whole air. The crowd stirred on the edges of their seats.

But from Gobi's eyes, there stood a little figure, some shadow that stared back at him. And the shadow said nothing on the projection rock, nothing from Gobi's tired and quivering and drained lips. It seemed that, suddenly, there was nothing Gobi could do. He practiced that week. And yet, he wasn't prepared. His mind went blank as he stared down at the crowd—the countless sweeping heads of the entire kingdom.

All Gobi knew was to listen to Yolia, and now the whole city watched him because he listened. He choked on his own breath because he listened. He stared at the shadow of his demise because he listened.

He'd been set up.

Why? He didn't know. *Why?*

He gulped once again and cleared his throat. The crowd began to muffle a soft rumble of feet and whispering lips.

Mikalla, on the ground and among everyone in the stadium, looked on, no longer in a trance or engaged.

He knew who stood on the projection rock. He recognized the flickering figure. It was Gobi. *But why?* He didn't know whether to feel envious or sad. *Is he screwing up? What's going on?*

Talking was strictly prohibited during the ceremony. His father leaned over to him. "Mikalla, what's he doing? Is this normal? Was this practiced?"

"No."

"Then what's he doing?"

"I have no idea." They all watched in anticipation.

But then, a voice poked through the air. Punctuating ears. Rattling thoughts. It was the voice of Gobi, trying his best to yell but sounding shrill.

"And the treacherous boy won. The treacherous boy proved to be victorious that day." The shadow raised one arm and turned his palm toward the sky. "And he continued on, happy and fulfilled. You are hereby dismissed."

But no one moved in the crowd. Just whispers. Just wide eyes. Just furrowed brows. Only the edges of the stadium seemed to slowly spill with Idazan people. The figure disappeared from the projection rock.

What's going on up there? Mikalla thought.

Yolia and Gobi faced one another. "How was that?" Yolia asked.

"You never said that was going to happen."

"That's what being The Conjurer is. It was all intentional, Gobi. It all culminated in another successful ceremony. Don't you worry. You did well."

Gobi bared his teeth. "It doesn't feel like I did."

Yolia tried to take him by the shoulder gently. Gobi fought his arm and retreated.

"Why'd you do that?"

"Do what?"

At that response, Gobi knew that something was afoot, something nefarious from Yolia. He eyed Yolia's every facial movement—every flick, every nerve impulse tracked and traced. *Did he want me to screw up?*

Something was off.

And then, Gobi stared at Yolia, but his mind pictured a different face. A different person: Mikalla.

He had to get rid of that weak little boy.

Gobi sweated while Yolia stayed still and calm under the cool night sky.

The impetuous boy turned around in a huff before Yolia could answer him.

I need to talk to the king before he does, Yolia thought.

Chapter 23

Gobi had a mission, and it raced in his heart and pumped through his veins. Red eyes poked out from his skull like vicious rubies. He went into the palace and hoped not to be seen until he hit the secret passage to the underground stairs. He came in clean and was ready to dirty his garments from the dust of the dark cavern. Only one goal with so many implications. Only one thing to see, and yet, so many possible outcomes.

If they haven't killed Mikalla yet, then what's the holdup? What's going on with these buffoons? I spent good money to wipe the floor with that artsy imbecile. The sabotage ends now....

His steps clopped and echoed on the rocky steps of the cavern. He noticed that one of the torches on the wall was out of its usual place. *That's odd.* Once he got deep and far away enough from the palace halls, he shouted at the men in masks. His voice was hoarse and hateful. Rushed and angered by the world that seemed to be closing in on him, just like the flitting light from above.

But there was a rank smell to the underground, and things were out of place. He noticed rags and dark garments, and the smell got worse—pungent and heavy to the nose. He made a face as his eyes adjusted to the dank light and the heavy fog of certain darkness. Light left. The perpetual nighttime of the underground closed in on him.

He thought he heard something. A quick sound. A fleeting rush. It then went away as soon as it came. The dust was defined, his steps loud. He looked around. Nothing on the walls besides torches—one missing. He paid little mind to his own mind, his own eyes, only thinking about the task at hand: pressuring the cloaks to kill Mikalla. And possibly to control them. And possibly to rule over them. And possibly to keep them under his grip so he could weaponize them against anyone that may threaten his position. There was so much to do. So much to say.

And then his nose caught a foul smell—*what is that?* Decay did not begin to describe the despairing scent that pervaded his nostrils. He smelled death, sin, and evil rot to its core.

Gobi grimaced and made a sound of disgust. He looked around some more, finally able to see definite shapes and objects.

The first object he spotted was a garment on the ground. Covered in blood. A glint then caught his eye. It was a lone gold coin stuck on top of the table in the middle of the cavern's entry space. He reached quickly to grab it.

He looked at the gold piece in his hand. It shimmered. But upon closer inspection, he saw something that disrupted the shimmer. It was a drop, a dollop of deep red. It looked and seemed like blood. A single drop. Holding it closer, he squinted. And as he did, something hard and blunt hit the back of his neck, throwing his head and sending his vision into a spiral. He wanted to run, but before he could act, he was struck again and again. His head. His torso. His neck. And soon, Gobi found himself where the garments were—stained and smelling of blood and death and dust. And as his eyes glazed over and his body went stiff before it went limp, he lay atop a pile of bodies, all of them cloaked and dusted with red drops and streams of blood. Battered, stabbed, and brutalized.

The bodies were still as stones. Gobi lay there as the newest of the collection of wide-eyed corpses.

And one figure stood above all of them, breathing heavily, heaving with a torch hanging by his side. He stared down, way down, at the blood and bodies. Gobi was only the final piece to the puzzle.

Kitan threw the torch onto the pile, wiped his hands, and went back up the stairs.

Chapter 24

"What do you mean Gobi didn't show up today?" Menizak was enraged. Thick anger smeared his brow.

Yolia stood his ground. He didn't know what to think. "He didn't. He wasn't there."

"You surely sent someone for him, right?"

"I did send for him after he didn't show for an hour."

"And he wasn't in his quarters?"

"No."

"Not in the palace or out on a walk?"

"It didn't appear so. I have a search party combing through all of the Inner Gardens to search for him. I'm not sure what they'll come up with, though."

The king turned away and put a hand to his gruff and thick face, his eyes sharp as spears. He looked out the window. They were in a vast parlor of the palace, far away and above the rest of the kingdom. Nothing seemed impossible to the king. The sun shone through the window. Nothing seemed out of the question. Everything seemed within bounds. He thought about Yolia. He thought about Mikalla, the mysterious boy. He thought about all the people that needed things and wanted certain outcomes that could never come true. And then he thought about all the outcomes that could be where people actually could tilt the table in their favor. *But who? And how?*

The king mused.

Yolia spoke up. "He could be anywhere, your highness. Really, anywhere."

"Then have your men search everywhere. Have them search far and wide. But..." and the king turned back around, "if he is not found or does not return, then...."

"Then what?"

"Then...." And the king was paralyzed. Strictly beholden to a frigid state. Unable to do or to say a thing.

"It's been all day, your highness. What is my duty if he's not found?"

Menizak's head spun. There was a correct answer that he held in his gut, which he did not wish to spew out just yet. He didn't want to go there. Gobi was his nephew. "Find him," the king said. "Find him and teach him, just as you've been doing." With Gobi installed as The Conjurer-in-training, he shored up more power. The king could control more with Gobi alive. He had a say. It would be harder if that lower noble boy had to be trained. And he would be, that is, if Gobi died or disappeared. This is to say that the king needed Gobi.

Having kin as The Conjurer versus that of *Yolia* would be helpful, would be advantageous, would be a nice luxury, and possibly, a need.

But maybe he could inject Mikalla with the same familial urgency as Gobi. Maybe he could have him under his influence. Yolia was already lost.

Yes, a fresh start would be better. A new Conjurer would be better than the free-spirited Yolia—the man that could finagle any story and influence anyone, everyone. He could have crowds on their feet or on a cloud. *But I still need a talented Conjurer. And dammit, they still need to be trained formally by Yolia. I need Yolia...for now.*

"And, if I can't find him?"

"Get the boy! The other boy!"

"Mikalla?"

"Whoever it is!"

Yolia tried not to smile. Mikalla was better. Mikalla was the one. Now, he actually had a chance.

"Understood, Your Highness."

Yolia turned and left.

***

Mikalla sat in his room. He had a school project to do. He didn't touch the project. He didn't touch anything besides the bed he sat on. Despite his nice parents and comfortable room, he lacked so much in his heart. He saw stars, wanting to throw a rock and hit them. But all he could do was hit the wet grass in front of him. He felt blind. But what did his feelings matter? All the good things that happened to him were outside his control. Most of the bad, too. Even his parents, who were so kind, were also extensions of powers beyond his control, his infantile grasp at nothing. His complexities were simple. He was born into the crowded middle. Just high enough for the opportunity. Just low enough to lack everything he saw.

He thought of the girl with brown hair. The thin one with the sharp eyes. But she paid no attention to him.

A single flame lit his room.

And then something happened that sprung him into action.

His father knocked on the door.

"What?"

"There's someone here to see you."

"I don't want to be seen." Mikalla wiped his eyes.

"It's The Conjurer."

Eyes widened. His neck flitted around. His room was dingy. "What?"

"Yolia. He's here to see you."

"Why?"

"That's for you guys to talk about."

"I'll be out in a second."

Mikalla thought for a while. *He died. He must've. Gobi must be...gone.* The weight of it struck Mikalla. Gobi was mean, snide, and rude. But him dying? Because of Oro's wish? Mikalla wrestled with the morality of it all.

He went downstairs to meet Yolia. Each step was a trip closer to his dreams.

***

They sat in Yolia's studio. It was a dark room with paintings all around. A huge oak desk was plotted on one side of the room. Yolia folded his hands, but Mikalla couldn't help but look around. There were paintings of battle scenes and lovers and mountains. Great scenes of heroism and hope. Sad and somber people, down and out. It was all incredible and it all sparked something in the boy with wide eyes and a world ahead of him.

Mikalla felt a burst of emotion, an animalistic compulsion to express himself from within. He had no control. He felt close to Yolia. He felt he could trust the man. "What am I?"

Yolia laughed. "That's something you're never going to figure out, Mikalla. I don't know who I am."

"Then how do I know what to do?"

"You don't. You create what you do. You, specifically, can create the world. Mikalla, if you're nothing else, then you're special."

But the boy could not take the compliment. He didn't believe Yolia's consolations.

"People don't think that. People seem to do what they want. But I'm not 'people.' Some seem to want to stop me or keep me down. I was just born and given all of this strife. What the hell is that? Like, why am I here in this room right now, with you? With me?"

"Well, why am I here? These questions are too big for you. So why wrestle with them?"

These questions are too big for me, Mikalla echoed in his head, *so why wrestle with them? Why wrestle with them?* The boy felt a sharpness inside of him subside and dull. He took a deep breath.

"Okay. I get it. I guess there's no reason to do so. But what do we do in place of the big questions?"

Yolia shifted in his seat. "We learn how to ask better questions. We create things that can stand and walk for a while. We can change things with our wills, Mikalla, no matter how small or large. Here—look at this rock." He reached his hand to grab a painted pebble at the corner of his desk. Grabbing it, he caressed it in his hand for a second, and then he put it in the center of the desk. He stared at Mikalla for a while.

"Why'd you do that?"

"No. No. No. No! That's not the question to ask, Mikalla. The question is this: what did I do?"

"So what'd you do?"

"I changed the course of history. And do you know what I did it with?"

"Your hand and a pebble?"

"No. Mikalla, I did it with my *will*. My own will. My will did it and moved the pebble. Mikalla, don't you see?"

"I see a pebble."

"No. You saw the power of will."

And then Yolia leaned in closer. He looked Mikalla dead in the eyes as the room seemed to darken, lights dimming, painted walls closing in. Yolia became stern and mean. He snapped at Mikalla and channeled a rage that the boy had never seen.

"You wanna know what the power of will is, Mikalla?"

The silent boy nodded with lips sealed shut.

"It's you, being in that seat, right there in front of me. It's you, being in my grasp right now. It's you being here. Hung by strings attached to my fingers. It's you being pushed and pulled at the will of *me*. Solely *me*. That's what will is. That's the power of will. I insert my will into the people of the entire kingdom—every single one of them—and they're *all* moved by it. They *all* love it." Yolia took a deep breath and leaned way back in his chair. "That's the power of stories. It's a source of intentional change. And intention, Mikalla, is *divine*."

"I understand."

"No, you don't. But you will. Eventually, you will."

"What am I going to do now?"

"You're going to get trained by me. You're going to become the next Conjurer."

Nick Oliveri

Chapter 25

A large, open-air hut sat newly built on the very outskirts of Idaza. The desert plains shone with blinding white sand. There was no horizon on that side of Idaza. There were no guards. No people or merchants. No gate. Just blankness away from everyone. Everyone except Kitan and his newfound crew, of course. He recruited multiple instructors from the school and builders and merchants and black-clad guards of his own. He paid them all handsomely. They wondered where the boy got his money, yet they paid that thought little mind as the gold continued to line their pockets. They constructed huts and worked on foreign substances, practicing some of the most forward sciences the city had ever seen. The merchants gathered resources that the scientists called for.

It was all Kitan's. It was all his vision that came to life. It was all there in and under the ceiling of the sandy hut. Being created and believed in, and worked on. They would begin to construct out of copper. And Kitan would continue to instruct them. That cycle of construction and instruction followed a violent and vigorous cyclone's path for years to come, hidden away in secrecy—Kitan's secret legion of creation. His own stories to build were slowly coming to life before his eyes.

He backed away and stared at the project before returning to his hidden hut in the dusty commons. *Patience.* He stared at the model on his rickety desk and smiled. He looked at the enormous pile of gold in the corner of his hut and quickly concealed it once again with a tattered blanket.

It was all coming together. Slowly. Surely. Copper would turn into metal. Cars would turn into trains, and rods would become tracks. Tracks. Cars. Connection. And if he owned the usage and construction of those vehicles, he owned the goods that were on them and even the kingdoms that used them. He could own it all one day.

Seamless. Seamless. Seamlessly connecting the many kingdoms of the Mesoas Valley. And then kings will fall as subjects to their own demise as commerce would take the front seat. Rise of the merchants. Their rise will be the rise of me. The rise of Kitan.

***

Later, the three converged in Oro's palatial quarters. The ceilings were as high as their hopes. Each of them was in good spirits, sitting up straight and energized. Oro spoke up first. Mikalla and Kitan both smiled for different reasons, waiting patiently for Oro to clear his dry throat and ask his question. His breath reeked of dry wine.

"And so, Gobi can't be found? Anywhere?"

"As far as we know."

Oro smiled. Kitan brightened his smug smirk. "And so you're being trained by him?"

"Yes. Fully." Mikalla couldn't believe the words that just left his mouth. He was then The Conjurer's apprentice. *The Conjurer's apprentice.*

"But where could Gobi be?"

"They must've disposed of him well," Kitan said.

"I guess so."

"So this is all good, right?"

Oro looked at both of them. Pride in his eyes shone through the windows to his soul, a genuine smile for his plan going well. "Yes. This is all good. Everything's going according to plan." Then he stood up and walked toward the window. His steps were shaky, taking a winding path instead of a straight one. Looking out, he said, "we are the next generation. Us three. We are going to be the power." And he turned around again excitedly, like a kid. "It's just us! We're the source. My father could never do this," he said bitterly. Rapid. "We're the ones. We have it. You're going to be The

Conjurer. You're going to be the Secretary of State. One, two, and three as one. A power base. Yes, a power base. None of the other Menizaks were ever able to do this. I did, though! I did!"

All three of them spied an open bottle of wine next to the chair where Oro once sat. He nearly ran over to it and took many swigs. "We're the ones!"

For a short time after that meeting, Mikalla continued to train, and Kitan continued to build out his vision.

Oro continued to drink.

Chapter 26

Jani took a walk outside. Her parents were panicking and continuing to panic over Gobi's disappearance. They both cried and fretted. They couldn't stop decaying right in front of Jani's eyes, all because one of their many children had disappeared forever. *He definitely died,* thought Jani. *Just give up. Let him go. My brother was a jerk, and that was all he was ever going to be.* But they continued to yell throughout the house and walk sullenly around the Inner Gardens.

As Jani stepped outside of the house unnoticed, she wore a bitter face and looked up at the sky. *They would never cry if I died. They would never fret or grieve if I disappeared.* A tear fell from her eye, sliding down her sharp jaw. She held her breath and kept walking and wiping her face, hiding it from everyone behind her cloak and her ashamed hands. She could barely see from her covering.

But out of the sketchy corner of her eye, she spotted a boy and a man. They walked alongside one another. It was that boy *from class. What's he doing with The Conjurer?* Jani's face melted into puzzlement. She looked at the side of Mikalla as he walked by and away from her. Naturally, she followed them.

"Um, hi. Hi!"

They both turned around. Yolia greeted Jani.

Mikalla just stood there. It felt like his eyes widened from the pressure coming from his heart, the heat of his gut melting his palms into carrying a film of sweat. He felt like melting or running away. He made eye contact with her. Shuddering. Vibrating. Breath froze despite the wildfire within. Shaking.

She held a slight smile. "Hi, Mikalla."

Does she know my name? She knows my name!

"Hi."

"Listen, we should hang out sometime."

"I-I'd love that." Mikalla looked blank and stolid, shivering violently but concealing it under a bright and detailed garment that danced and glimmered with his nervous movements.

"Sounds good. I'll see you around."

They both went their separate ways, and for the first time in a while, Jani smiled with her full teeth showing. Her tears faded as she saw the opportunity unfold in her mind. That boy seemed easy to manipulate, to get close to, and control. *I can have him. Maybe I already do. And then his influence will be mine. This is the way. This is my way. My garbage family will never exceed me. They could never do what I do. They don't look like me. They don't have my mind or my drive. I'm so much better than them or anyone. That boy is mine. His job is mine. I can control the controller.*

Jani spat on the ground as pictures of her brother faded forever. She pictured her parents suffering as she watched. "You should've paid attention to me."

And then she walked on through the peaceful Inner Gardens, tears dried under the sun. *Life isn't fair, but fairness is for fools.*

Chapter 27

The sun went down in Idaza, revealing a covering of night perforated by dusk's pink splatters and twilight's purple smears. By the clarity of the stars, the moon looked down on the kingdom and frowned.

Nick Oliveri

Author Bio

Nick Oliveri is a 23-year-old, Ukrainian-born, Kirkus-Recommended author of seven novels and an ebook of poetry. He is often dubbed as a controversial creator of transgressive fiction and genre-bending literature.

Nick treasures the unique potential behind every person's story and values sharing those tales with the world. Skilled at crafting sentences that bring his characters and their narratives to life, he is passionate about the beauty the written word has to offer.

Oliveri draws from a unique set of creators that have inspired him throughout the years. These include Jean-Michel Basquiat, Vladimir Nabokov, Stephen King, and Lil Wayne.

Nick is a former startup co-founder dedicated to the onset of the circular economy. Born in Ukraine but having grown up in Massachusetts, Nick happily resides on the Monterey Peninsula in Marina, CA, and loves wine, hockey, surfing, philosophy, art, and of course, reading and writing.

Printed in the USA
CPSIA information can be obtained
at www.ICGtesting.com
LVHW040533260624
784023LV00004B/318